Hazel stumbled to each tent and wrenched open the flaps. "Jackson, where are you?"

Mitchell assisted in her search, but as he'd suspected, no boys were anywhere to be found.

"Help," a faint voice cried from the bushes.

Mitchell stooped low and checked under the branches. A man stared back at him. Mitchell dragged him out of his concealed spot. "What happened?"

"Where is my son? Why were you hiding?"

"We were attacked," the man said as he held his abdomen, blood dripping through his fingers. "The boys and I were coming up from the river when we saw them shoot Dave. I told the boys to run, but before I could go with them, someone stabbed me and pushed me into the bushes. Then I passed out."

"My boy is out there alone?"

"We'll find him, Hazel. I promise." Mitchell unfastened his radio and requested emergency services for Aaron.

The boys were in danger not only from a gunman but from a forest full of wildlife, including bears and cougars.

It was up to Mitchell to find them.

Darlene L. Turner is an award-winning author who lives with her husband, Jeff, in Ontario, Canada. Her love of suspense began when she read her first Nancy Drew book. She's turned that passion into her writing and believes readers will be captured by her plots, inspired by her strong characters and moved by her inspirational message. Visit Darlene at www.darlenelturner.com, where there's suspense beyond borders.

Books by Darlene L. Turner

Love Inspired Suspense

Border Breach
Abducted in Alaska
Lethal Cover-Up
Safe House Exposed
Fatal Forensic Investigation
Explosive Christmas Showdown
Alaskan Avalanche Escape
Mountain Abduction Rescue

Visit the Author Profile page at LoveInspired.com.

MOUNTAIN ABDUCTION RESCUE

DARLENE L. TURNER

LOVE INSPIRED SUSPENSE
INSPIRATIONAL ROMANCE

LOVE INSPIRED SUSPENSE
INSPIRATIONAL ROMANCE

Recycling programs
for this product may
not exist in your area.

ISBN-13: 978-1-335-59758-8

Mountain Abduction Rescue

For questions and comments about the quality of this book, please contact us at CustomerService@Harlequin.com.

Love Inspired
22 Adelaide St. West, 41st Floor
Toronto, Ontario M5H 4E3, Canada
www.LoveInspired.com

Printed in U.S.A.

It is of the Lord's mercies that we are not consumed, because his compassions fail not. They are new every morning: great is thy faithfulness.
—*Lamentations* 3:22-23

For Tamela
Thank you for being the best agent ever.

Acknowledgments

To Jeff: Where do I begin? You're always there for me and have been supportive in my transition of retiring and beginning my full-time writing career. You are a treasure from God and I love you more each day.

To my family: Thank you for your continual encouragement. I love you.

To my writer friends: Thank you for always being available to brainstorm, help me find the right word and talk me off the ledge. LOL.

To my editor, Tina James, and my agent, Tamela Hancock Murray: You are both amazing and I'm thankful God has put us together.

Most of all, to Jesus, my Savior and Friend: Thank You for knowing the best path for my life. May I always give You the honor and glory.

ONE

Park warden Hazel Hoyt adjusted her duty belt and radio before stepping onto the porch of her father's ranch just outside Micmore National Park, Alberta. Smoke assaulted her nose, and a rush of angst tensed her muscles as she observed the distant wildfire cloud blanketing the region next to her beloved Micmore Mountain. The inferno would soon reach her if the unit crews didn't contain the beast. One thought plagued her mind.

It was only a matter of time before the Rocky Mountain Firebug struck her park.

The serial arsonist had been setting fires all along the Rocky Mountain ranges and various buildings within towns. Three firefighters had lost their lives, including a well-known chief. How many more would perish before authorities apprehended the madman?

Hazel's radio crackled. "Be on the lookout," dispatch said. "Suspicious activity around Micmore National Park."

Her heart hitched. "Shari, what does that mean?"

"Hey, Hazel," the motherly fifty-something said. "We're still trying to get an update. Will let you know when I find out more."

"Copy that. Heading in now." Hazel clicked off.

She loved her park and would do anything to safeguard

it—even put her life on the line. Her job included law enforcement as well as protecting the area, wildlife and campers against predators.

"I heard Shari's radio call. Keep your eyes peeled out there today. This guy will target Micmore and our town any day now. You understand?"

Hazel turned at the sound of her father's stern voice. Supervisor Frank Hoyt demanded allegiance and intimidated everyone around him, including his children. Hazel's strangled grip on the wooden railing increased, whitening her knuckles. Did he really think her incapable of doing her job? He had trained her, after all.

Park life was in her blood, along with her four brothers and three sisters. Growing up with a park supervisor as a father had instilled a love of outdoor life in them. He now made all the decisions for the parks around the region. The authority had gone to his head, and he'd become insufferable.

Hazel suppressed a sigh and removed her keys. "Gotta head in. Jackson's troop is moving their campsite to higher ground today."

Her father had insisted Hazel enroll her eight-year-old in summer camp. "He needs an early start sleeping out in the wild," her father had said. "It's how I taught all of you."

Right. Like we had a choice.

Hazel could tell the thought of camping without her had scared her son, but she'd talked him into it. Hazel caved to Frank Hoyt…yet again.

When will I ever stand up to him?

"Talk to you later, Dad." She bounded down the steps to her pickup truck.

"Remember, keep your—"

Hazel opened the door and turned. "Eyes to the skies

and ears in nature. I got it, Dad." His saying was ingrained in her brain. She gritted her teeth.

I know how to do my job.

She hopped into her truck and drove down the long, winding driveway, glancing in the rearview mirror at the ranch disappearing in the distance. As much as she wanted to get out from under her father's tyrannical thumb, she loved Hoyt Hideaway Ranch. Plus, Jackson enjoyed living with his doting grandmother. Being a single parent had proven difficult for Hazel, and her mother, Erica Hoyt, had been a lifesaver.

Hazel set aside thoughts of the Hoyt family and made her way to her park station. She drove into its lot at the same time as her coworker, Nora Martin. They'd known each other since grade school and Hazel had often confided in her friend about their domineering supervisor, Frank Hoyt.

Hazel exited her vehicle. "Morning, Nora. Looks like another warm day."

"Sure does." She pointed to the horizon. "Not going to help the fire over there."

Hazel put on her cowboy-like, park-warden hat. "Nope, and let's pray it doesn't spread toward us."

"And that Firebug stays out of our park and town." Nora opened her trunk.

Locals dubbed the Rocky Mountain Firebug simply "Firebug" and it caught on. He had targeted the area surrounding her small town of Bowhead Springs near Banff, Alberta. Deep into the Rocky Mountains. Authorities had failed to apprehend him, but had released details on his signature, which Hazel had memorized.

Nora strapped her knapsack on her back. "I'm coming with you today. Need to check the area for safety concerns." She took pride in her role as safety specialist where she provided visitor-risk management to the team.

"Excellent. Let me gather the rest of my equipment first." She eyed the stables. "How about we take the horses?"

"Yes. I've been itching to ride Thunder."

A new voice joined the conversation. Shari. "Hazel, I have an update for you."

Hazel pressed her shoulder radio button. "Go ahead. What are we looking for?"

"A scout leader reported a suspicious figure around their campsite. Micmore unit's crew leader is en route. Just in case."

Hazel's pulse escalated, and she grabbed Nora's arm. "Jackson's troop is camping."

Nora patted Hazel's hand. "There are a bunch of troops out there. He's okay. Get your stuff and let's go."

Hazel nodded and headed into her station.

After adding her weapon to her belt and necessities into her knapsack, Hazel mounted her favorite horse, Chestnut. She rubbed his mane. "Time to work, bud." Hazel gently nudged her legs into Chestnut and the animal responded by trotting after Nora on Thunder.

"Can we head to Jackson's campsite? I can't get in touch with Dave." Hazel had tried numerous times to contact the troop leader since leaving her father's ranch, but he wasn't answering her radio call. Concern corded her neck muscles. *Lord, please protect my boy.*

"Sure, which way?" Nora asked.

"Toward Buttercup Trail." Hazel steered Chestnut down the path, taking them deeper into the park.

Moments later, a rustling in the trees caught her attention before a hooded figure passed by her peripheral vision, shifting from tree to tree. Something wasn't right. She eased her reins back and Chestnut stopped. Hazel turned to Nora, placing her index finger on her lips. "Someone is ahead," she whispered. "Stay here."

Hazel knew Nora could take care of herself, but Hazel was the one with a weapon. She dismounted and placed her hand on her gun. She never drew it out unless absolutely necessary. Especially because of what happened the last time she discharged her 9mm. Poachers had infiltrated her park and killed a coworker after her defensive shot missed. A day she'd never forget.

She inched through the woods where she'd seen the figure hide behind a tree, and peered into the small clearing.

The hooded man bent next to a Douglas fir and withdrew a small paper bag from his pocket, stuffing a candle inside.

The Rocky Mountain Firebug's signature.

Hazel failed to suppress her gasp.

The suspect rose and turned, revealing a masked man.

She whipped out her gun and pressed her radio button. "Firebug spotted in the north clearing of Buttercup Trail. Send backup now."

"I'm coming, Hazel," Nora's voice yelled from the radio.

"No, you're not armed." Hazel raised her weapon and advanced into the opening. "Give it up, man," she called out. "Constables will be swarming this place in minutes. There's nowhere to run."

Nora appeared to the right of Hazel, skulking through the trees.

Lord, protect my friend.

"Retribution will happen and you can't stop me." The man's snarling words spoke volumes. "Back away, Warden."

Retribution? For what? The questions tumbled through her mind as she lifted her gun higher. "Not on my watch. Hoyts never back down."

"So I've heard. Hoyts are insufferable."

What does that mean?

She didn't recognize the man's voice, so how did Firebug know her family?

"Micmore unit's leader and his crew are on their way to you, Hazel," dispatch said.

Get them here fast, Lord.

Firebug took out a lighter and lit the bag. "Too late. Time for your precious park to burn and those firefighters to die."

"No!" Nora yelled. She circled around him and bulldozed into the man.

He tripped and dropped the bag as he fell to the ground, entangling himself in a crocodile roll with Nora.

Flames ignited the grass and slithered into the fir trees.

God, no. Save our park.

Hazel bolted forward, trying to get a clear shot, but her coworker blocked her line of sight. "Nora, move."

Firebug shoved Nora into one of their many park benches. She hit her head and stilled. Was she conscious?

"Nora!" Hazel prayed her coworker was okay, but the fire was already spreading to the next tree. It was time to act or all would be lost.

Once again, she raised her weapon, and aimed. She fired, but her shot went wide.

Stupid, Hazel.

Her nerves had taken over moments before she pulled the trigger, as she remembered the last time she'd missed her target.

The Rocky Mountain Firebug catapulted himself forward and tackled her.

She dropped her gun and tried to get free from his tight grip, but her tiny frame was no match for the enormous man's strength. With her free hand, she fumbled with his mask, hoping to expose his face. However, his powerful grip kept her anchored.

"Nice try." His raspy voice personified evil.

Movement and Chestnut's whinny alerted them to company. Help had arrived.

Hazel squirmed in his hold. "I will stop you if it's the last thing I do."

"I'm on a mission and no one will get in my way." Firebug extracted a jackknife and hit the button to release the blade, holding it high. "Time to say goodbye, Hazel."

She attempted to block his aim, but it was useless. She was going to die.

Hazel mustered courage and swatted at his hand, but not quick enough.

His blade punched into her side.

Pain exploded and black spots danced in her vision.

A motorized vehicle sounded nearby, then the engine cut out.

"Stop!" a voice yelled.

The weight from Firebug's muscular body lifted, and his quick footfalls shot toward the forest.

Hazel turned her diminishing gaze and caught sight of the man headed toward her.

Her best friend's older brother—and her first crush.

"Mitchell?"

She could say no more as searing pain registered and plunged her into murky darkness.

Micmore Wildfire Unit's crew leader, Mitchell Booth, dashed forward after hearing his sister's best friend's cry, ignoring pursuit of the Rocky Mountain Firebug. Her safety and the raging flames were his first concern. He dropped by her side and placed his fingers on her neck, then checked her breathing. Both strong, which told him she'd probably passed out from the pain of her wound. However, she required help…and so did he. He unclipped his radio. "Booth here. Smokey, I'm on the Buttercup Trail. Dispatch, send paramedics. Stat." He gave additional location details and observed the other unconscious woman. "Two females need medical assistance."

"Copy that," dispatch said. "Deploying now."

Thankfully, his team had also entered the park and weren't far behind. They'd been on alert ever since Firebug had set the last wildfire closer to their location. The arsonist had been plaguing the area for weeks and authorities were still no further ahead in identifying him.

Mitchell quickly dragged both Hazel and her coworker farther away from the flames. He applied pressure to Hazel's wound and prayed his team would arrive fast. The flames were spreading, but he had to protect his little sister's best friend.

She stirred and coughed as she struggled to speak. "Stop. Fire."

It was just like Hazel to be more concerned about the park than herself. He remembered how much she loved the national parks in Alberta. He placed her hands on top of her wound. "Apply pressure. Paramedics are on their way."

He stood and unhooked the hose attached to his backpack pump, then sprayed the fire. He had to work fast to contain the spread.

Firefighting was in Mitchell's blood, and when he'd seen the ad for wildland firefighters in his hometown area, he immediately applied for the job. He'd been working in Ontario and seized the opportunity to move back to the mountains—his first love. Protecting the wilderness had been his calling ever since he was ten years old.

Five minutes later, pounding footsteps hustled into the small clearing. "Boomer! Orders?"

Help had arrived. Mitchell turned at the sound of Smokey's voice. Each member of his twenty-person unit had a nickname. They'd named Mitchell *Boomer* when they found out he'd returned to Alberta—like a boomerang. "Smokey, get your team digging a control line for containment." Mitchell turned to a female. "Princess, help our victims until the paramedics arrive. Apply pressure to Hazel's stab wound." He hated the woman's nickname, but she loved it and kept correcting him when he called her by her real name.

The towering thirty-something nodded and hurried to Hazel's side.

Mitchell extinguished more flames. "Okay, team. Do what you do best. Let's contain this."

After cutting off further spread, Mitchell approached Hazel. Paramedics had treated her and taken Nora away for more care, but Hazel had refused to leave the area. Thankfully, the paramedic had stopped the bleeding on her side and bandaged her wound. He said it wasn't deep, and her attacker had just missed a vital area. She'd be okay, however, he warned her to get to the hospital anyway.

Mitchell sat on the bench. "Hazel, why aren't you taking the paramedic's advice?"

"Good to see you too, Mitchell." Her contorted expression revealed her annoyance at the question.

"Sorry, good to see you again. How long has it been?"

"Since you left and stood me up for my prom?" She held up her index finger. "Wait, I saw you briefly at your mom's funeral but you avoided me."

Ouch. How could he have forgotten that he'd left so quickly, after promising to take her to the high school dance when no other boys would? He'd taken pity on her and relented to his sister's demand. Although, looking at her now, years later, made him question why he had hesitated. Her girlish, nerdy looks had blossomed into beauty.

He set the thought aside and focused on their conversation. "I'm sorry Brock didn't tell you." His best friend at the time had promised to contact her when Mitchell hadn't been able to get in touch with his sister.

"I was humiliated and left standing at the high school entrance holding your boutonniere. The other girls laughed at me." She paused. "I didn't find out until later that you left Alberta quickly."

"This really isn't the time to discuss this, but Brock was supposed to tell you an unexpected firefighter training opportunity came up and I had to fly out that night." He took off his helmet and rubbed his soot-covered face. "You didn't answer my question. Why are you not going to the hospital?"

"I promised the paramedic I would go later. Jackson needs me." She eased herself up. "We have to find him, Mitchell. Can you help?"

His sister, Bree, had told him about Hazel's son, but not the entire story of what had happened to the boy's father. Mitchell popped to his feet. "What's going on?"

"Jackson is out with his troop, camping. I've been trying to get in touch with his leaders, Dave and Aaron. However, neither is picking up. Something's happened." Her lip quivered. "And there's a madman in our park."

"Do you know the troop's last location?"

"Yes, but they were moving camps this morning. It was a two-night excursion."

"How old is Jackson?" he asked.

"Eight. Before you say anything, his grandfather insisted he attend summer camp."

"Ah. The mighty Frank Hoyt speaks." Mitchell remembered the man's dictatorship. It was why most of Hazel's brothers had left the area. They were tired of his forceful ways.

"Please. Can you help?"

"How far away is their last known camp?"

"About a kilometer. We'll get there faster if we take Chestnut and Thunder." She gestured toward his UTV. "Plus, the terrain isn't the best for your vehicle."

Mitchell's team had relocated the horses farther down the trail to keep them from the smoke fumes. "You okay to ride, though?"

"I'll be fine. Let's go." She bent to pick up her weapon and shuffled toward the path.

Ugh. The stubborn streak he remembered had surfaced. Once Hazel Hoyt set her mind to something, no one could alter her determination.

A trait he respected. But now, she was still weak.

"Let me help you." He put his arm around her, guiding her to where her tethered horse stood.

Hazel freed herself from his hold and grabbed Chestnut's reins. "I can do it." She adjusted her hat and inserted her foot into the stirrup, hoisting her body up. She choked in a breath and fell back down, dropping the reins.

Mitchell scurried forward and caught her. "Careful or your wound will bleed again." He helped her into the saddle before handing her the straps.

She accepted them and turned her gaze to the trail. "Let's go." She clucked and nudged Chestnut forward.

"Hold on. It's been years since I've ridden. I need to get Smokey to pick up the UTV and contact my boss to let him know I'm helping you." He quickly gave his coworker instructions before untethering Thunder. He mounted and nudged the horse's flank. The horse jolted, throwing Mitchell back in the saddle. "Whoa." He righted himself and gripped the reins tighter.

Hazel turned. "Come on, Cowboy. Keep up." She laughed, then winced and clutched her side. "This way." She steered her horse to the right.

Five minutes later, they reached her son's campsite.

What Mitchell saw made a cold sweat break out on his heated skin. Smoke rising from the diminishing campfire. Food strewn across the grass. Multiple lawn chairs knocked over, indicating a struggle. The camp appeared to be abandoned, though the tents still remained.

His gaze shot from the farthest tent to a figure on the ground. A man lay motionless, a gunshot wound to the head.

"Dave!" Hazel's cry pierced the early morning hours and echoed throughout the woods.

Mitchell dismounted and helped Hazel from her horse. He brought her into an embrace. "I'm so sorry."

She wiggled free and stumbled to each tent, wrenching open the flaps. "Jackson, where are you?"

Mitchell assisted in her search, but as he'd suspected, no boys were anywhere to be found.

"Help," a faint voice cried from the bushes.

Mitchell stooped low and checked under the branches. A man stared back at him.

Hazel dropped to her knees. "Aaron?"

Mitchell dragged him out of his concealed spot. "What happened?"

"Where is my son? Why were you hiding?" Hazel laced her questions with contempt.

Mitchell understood. Her son was missing.

"We were attacked," the man said as he held his abdomen, blood dripping through his fingers. "The boys and I were coming up from the river after an early morning fishing trip when we saw them shoot Dave. I told the boys to run, but before I could go with them, someone stabbed me and pushed me into the bushes. Then I passed out." He held up a shattered cell phone in his other hand. "Broke my phone too."

"My boy is out there alone?" Hazel fell backward onto her heels.

"We'll find him, Hazel. I promise." Mitchell unfastened his radio and requested emergency services for Aaron. Determination squared his shoulders. He would let nothing happen to her son.

The boys were in danger not only from a madman but from a forest full of wildlife, including bears and cougars.

Mitchell gazed upward. Dark clouds now intermingled with the smoky wildfire blanket, forming an ominous cover.

Now the boys would have to contend with a thunderstorm. Alone and lost in the wilderness.

Not a good combination.

It was up to Mitchell to find them.

TWO

Hazel's heartbeat amplified tenfold at the thought of her son being chased by an unknown assailant in the unpredictable wilderness. She doubled over not only from the sudden surge of pain from her wound but from the anger boiling inside her. Anger at herself for sending Jackson on the trip. Anger at her father for insisting he go. Her wheezing breaths came out in a short, syncopated rhythm. *Breathe, Hazel. Breathe.* She inhaled deeply to slow the panic attack. Her heightened emotions would not help her son. Had the Rocky Mountain Firebug taken Jackson? No, wait. Aaron had said *them.*

She stiffened and turned to Aaron. "You said *them.* How many attacked the camp?"

"Two. Both with hoodies. Don't know anything else." Aaron clutched his stomach. "I need medical attention. Now." The man bit his lip and looked away.

Hazel's gaze snapped to Mitchell's. From his expression, she knew he had the same thought.

Aaron wasn't telling them everything.

Hazel had to probe deeper. "They're on their way." Ignoring the pain, she squatted next to the man. "Listen, I realize you're scared, but we need your help. Can you describe the men?"

"Um...both male. One tall, one short."

"Did you see their faces?" Mitchell asked.

"No, they wore masks."

Did Firebug have accomplices?

Something niggled at Hazel. Something she'd missed. She paced around the tents and looked for any type of clues. "Which tents are yours and Dave's?"

Aaron pointed.

Hazel entered Dave's and rummaged through his belongings. Nothing out of the ordinary. She switched to Aaron's.

"What are you looking for?" Mitchell asked as he followed her into the second tent.

"His story isn't sitting right with me."

"Agreed. He's withholding information." Mitchell opened a knapsack and rifled through it. "Wait, check this out." He held up a burner cell phone.

"Didn't he break his phone? Why would he have two?"

Mitchell's eyes narrowed. "Time to find out the truth." He stomped from the tent and over to Aaron, raising the device. "What aren't you telling us? Why do you have two phones? Where are those boys?"

Aaron recoiled and scrambled backward, holding his wound. "I—I can't…"

Hazel moved into the man's personal space. "You can't what? Tell us what you did."

He squeezed his lips into an impregnable line and shook his head.

His silence spoke volumes. He wasn't budging.

Perhaps reason would help persuade him to share the information he withheld. "Aaron, please. My son and those boys are out there alone. You realize what our wilderness is like. Plus we just had an altercation with the Rocky Mountain Firebug."

The leader's eyes bulged. He opened his mouth, then clamped it shut.

Hazel tugged on Mitchell's arm, leading him away. "We have to do something," she whispered. "Every minute those boys are out there, the more they are in danger."

Mitchell folded his arms across his chest. "What do you want me to do? Force him to talk?"

"No, of course not. But—"

A rustling on the trail beside the campsite interrupted them, revealing they weren't alone.

Hazel's hand flew to her weapon.

Supervisor Frank Hoyt appeared in the clearing. "Why aren't you out searching yet, Hazel?"

Great, he was all she needed right now. His overbearing presence made the strongest of men scatter like ants from their disturbed colonies.

"Dad, Dave is dead, and Aaron is withholding information. We're trying to get more details."

Mitchell inched closer to Hazel as if displaying a unified front.

He held out his hand. "Good to see you again, sir. Hazel is doing everything she can to bring her son home."

Wow...you don't realize who you're dealing with, do you?

Mitchell had been away for years and obviously had forgotten about her father's power. But good for him for standing up to a man no one dared to cross.

Supervisor Hoyt hesitated but finally took Mitchell's hand. "Good to see you, Mitchell. When did you get back into town?"

"Few months ago. I'm leader of the Micmore Wildfire Unit crew."

"Well, I've heard that crew is reckless. They need some harsh discipline."

Really, Dad?

Hazel studied Mitchell's face, but the man remained stoic. *Good for you.* "Dad, see what information you can get out of Aaron. He knows something about the attack." She might as well use her father's rough demeanor to their advantage.

Her father's expression hardened. "You bet I will." He marched over to where Aaron sat and hauled him to his feet by the collar. "Tell me where my grandson is or you'll live to regret it."

"I—I don't know." The man's stammered words revealed his fear of the powerful supervisor.

Her father poked his finger in Aaron's chest. "My daughter says you're hiding something. What do you know? Did you let them take those boys?"

Before Aaron could respond, a crowd entered the campsite. Constables and emergency services had arrived.

A male paramedic raced to where her father held Aaron by the throat. "Sir, let me examine the patient."

"Hold on a sec, Evan," her father said. "He has information we need." He tugged Aaron closer. "Tell me and we'll let Paramedic Carson take care of you."

"They—they said he'd kill me if I talked."

What did that mean? Pounding exploded in Hazel's temples as her neck muscles knotted.

She stepped next to Aaron, forcing her father to step aside. "We'll get the local authorities to protect you. Help me save my son and those boys."

His shoulders slumped. "I'm sorry. I'm broke, and they promised cash."

"What did you do, Aaron?" Her father's stern voice boomed.

"I was told to look the other way when they came calling, but in the end, I couldn't do it. That's why I instructed the boys to run and the men stabbed me before taking off after them."

An object hanging on a branch behind Aaron swayed in the breeze. A hat. Was that— She ran over and snatched the troop hat, turning it over. She gasped as she spotted the name written under the brim. Jackson Hoyt. She waved the hat in Aaron's face. "My son is missing. How long ago did this attack happen?" Her questions squeaked out through her tight throat.

"About thirty minutes."

That meant the boys had been wandering since then. Hazel clenched Jackson's hat. *Protect my son, Lord.*

"Why did they want the boys?" Mitchell asked.

Aaron gestured toward Hazel. "Because of her."

Hazel's legs buckled, and she teetered.

Mitchell caught her before she fell. "I've got you."

Questions fogged Hazel's mind. "Why did they target—"

A memory flashed from Firebug's attack.

Her jaw dropped as stabbing pains pricked her wound. She inhaled sharply and covered her side. *Lord, I don't have time to tend to my injury. Keep me strong.*

Mitchell held her tighter. "What is it, Hazel?"

His smoky scent from extinguishing the fire lingered on his clothes, but she ignored it. "He called me Hazel."

"Who?"

"Firebug. Right before he stabbed me. He said 'Time to say goodbye, Hazel.' This attack was personal, but why?"

"Did you get a look at his face?" Mitchell asked.

"No, I tried to pull his mask down, but he was too strong. I didn't recognize his voice either." Hazel wiggled out of his hold and once again marched over to Aaron, standing eye to eye with the man. "What do you mean, because of me? Is this connected to the Rocky Mountain Firebug? Do you know who he is?"

Silence.

"Tell me," Hazel yelled.

Aaron startled at her firm tone. "Yes, Firebug wanted your son but didn't say why. I can tell you who he is, but you have to promise to keep me safe."

"You're on thin ice, Aaron," her father said. "Tell us what you know. Now."

Hazel rubbed the man's arm. "We'll make sure no one harms you. I promise." Not that she was a cop, but she'd do anything to get her son back.

"He's—"

A flash from the tree borderline caught Hazel's attention seconds before a shot echoed throughout the park.

Aaron dropped, a gunshot to the temple.

"No!" Hazel screamed.

Mitchell shoved her to the ground, covering her body to protect her from the gunman in the trees.

The Rocky Mountain Firebug used a bullet to silence Aaron instead of a fire.

A question remained in Hazel's brain.

How was she connected to the madman?

Mitchell's head throbbed from the gunshot blast as he huddled over Hazel. His erratic pulse matched hers in tempo. He breathed in and out, lengthening the time with each exhale. Shouts and pounding footsteps sounded around them. The constables had reacted to the gunfire.

"Mitchell, let me up," Hazel said.

He rolled off her and eased himself into a standing position.

She stood and unleashed her gun, raising it in the direction from where the shot had come. "Anyone see the shooter?"

"Constable Porter pursued the assailant." Supervisor Hoyt pointed to Aaron. "Whatever additional information he had is gone." He withdrew his radio. "I'm going to light a fire under the search party. We're running out of time."

"Dad, wait. Take this to the search-and-rescue dogs." She handed him Jackson's hat. "It could help."

Frank nodded and walked away.

Mitchell rubbed his temples, a clear indicator of a storm brewing. Who needed a barometer when he had his head to warn him of bad weather? "Hazel, you okay? I didn't mean to haul you to the ground so hard. Just wanted to protect you."

She pursed her lips. "I'm fine, and I can take care of myself."

He raised his hands. "I realize that. Sorry, natural reaction. You know. Male protects female. Won't happen again."

She chuckled, her smile illuminating her beautiful face.

How had he not seen her beauty before now? Was it because he'd been so focused on the fact she was two years younger and Bree's best friend? The nerdy Hazel had followed him around endlessly to the point of irritation. But this older, attractive woman with the wide hazel eyes prickled his emotions.

Didn't matter.

Ivy Foster had spoiled him from pursuing another relationship. Her obsession with him after he ended things had turned deadly. She'd not only broken his heart but almost killed him. Literally. He had vowed never to get involved again. His heart couldn't take it, and Hazel wouldn't fall for Bree's brother anyway—not after he'd left her dateless for her prom. Even though he had had a valid reason, would she even trust him again?

He cleared his throat in an attempt to switch his mind to the situation at hand. *Focus, Mitch.*

Her father returned to the group, holding a map. "Okay, I've spoken with SAR and set the search party in motion. Let's go to the picnic table and coordinate our efforts."

Mitchell and Hazel followed him to the table, sitting beside each other with her father on the opposite side.

Frank spread out the map. "I'm old school. None of this tablet stuff." He pointed. "We're here." Then he tapped on different locations around the park. "We've sent units here, here and here."

Hazel leaned closer and placed her finger on the map. "Okay, but what about this spot, Dad?" She gestured to a trail that led to a river.

Her father's face twisted. "You really think the boys would have gone there? Jackson knows how swift the river current is. That's not a logical route and it's too far north."

"I'm not sure a group of eight-year-olds are thinking logically when they're being chased," Mitchell said. "I agree with Hazel. We need to cover every region of the park."

Supervisor Frank Hoyt slammed his palm down. "You are not in charge here. I am."

Oops. The man's sharp tone proved Mitchell had overstepped.

And he was correct. Mitchell had no say in the matter.

Hazel stood. "Mitchell's right. We can't risk not covering the entire park. Dad, I know how my son thinks. Water has always fascinated him. I'm going in that direction and I'm taking Chestnut. It will speed up my approach. I'll report in every thirty minutes." She stuffed her hat firmly in place and headed toward her horse.

Mitchell jumped to his feet. "Wait, Hazel. I'll go too. Let's be smart about this and get supplies first. We won't help the boys by being unprepared."

Hazel turned. "Don't you have to guide your unit and watch the forest fires?"

He unclipped his radio and raised it. "I can monitor with this. Besides, the arsonist is out there, and I'm not letting you go alone. We catch Firebug, we end all these fires. I'll check in with my team for an update, then—"

Constable Zeke Porter bounded around the corner. "Shooter escaped. No sign of him."

Frank bolted off the picnic bench and charged at the constable. "How could you let that happen? The man is after my grandson."

Hazel darted forward and yanked her father back. "Dad, it's not his fault."

He turned on his daughter. "How can you remain so calm? Your son's life is at stake. Don't you care?"

She stumbled backward as if he'd slapped her across the face.

How could the man treat his daughter so harshly? Especially at a time like this.

"Sir, with all due respect, how can you say that?" Mitchell asked.

Frank waggled his finger in Mitchell's face. "This is none of your concern. Stay in your own lane or I'll report you to your leader."

Wow. Mitchell couldn't imagine what had caused this man to become so bitter and condescending. Or had his rise in ranks gone to his head?

Hazel grazed Mitchell's arm. "Let's go. There's no use arguing with him." She walked away.

After gearing up and requesting Smokey update their leader with the latest information, Mitchell mounted Thunder. He and Hazel headed north on Whispering Creek Trail.

Forty-five minutes passed, and other than yelling Jackson's name, she'd not uttered a word since they began their search.

Mitchell nudged Thunder, and he guided the horse to get in step beside Hazel. "You okay?"

"Fine."

But her flattened lips told him otherwise.

"I don't believe you."

She turned to him. "Dad just infuriates me so much. I can't do anything right."

"He shouldn't have said what he did. I can tell by the look on your face how much you love your son."

Hazel stared at him before averting her gaze back to the trail. "Thanks. Dad has to be right about everything."

"Has he always been that harsh?"

"Mostly." She brought Chestnut to a stop. "Let's check our progress on the map." She fished it out of her vest pocket and pointed. "Okay, we've come this far and there's still no sign of the boys."

"How many are in the group?"

"Five, including Jackson." Her lip quivered.

He squeezed her shoulder. "He's okay. We'll find him." Once again, Mitchell yelled Jackson's name.

But only the birds answered.

Her radio crackled. "We've had a sighting by a hiker near Whispering River," Shari said.

Hazel straightened in her saddle. "See? I was right." She pressed her button. "Warden Hoyt here. We're proceeding to the canoe rack by the river. Keep me posted."

"Copy that," dispatch said.

Hazel tucked the map away. "Let's go." She clucked and nudged Chestnut forward, steering him onto a side path. "We'll get there quicker this way," she yelled.

He matched her speed and followed her down the densely wooded path.

Moments later, she leaned back and tugged the reins. "Whoa, boy." The horse stopped. She dismounted, tethering Chestnut at the top of a path. "We need to proceed on foot. Leave the horses here." She kissed Chestnut's forehead. "You'll be okay, bud. We'll be back."

She hustled down the wooden plank toward the river.

"Wait up!" He climbed off Thunder and quickly tied the reins to a tree, gathering his knapsack before following her.

"Mitchell, hurry."

Her frantic cry propelled him forward. He ran down the plank.

She squatted near a rack of canoes beside a small shanty.

"What is it?" He reached her and dropped to the ground.

She held up a small, lightweight blue jacket. "This is Jackson's. He left it here for me to find. Something I'd taught him to do if he was ever lost."

A bread crumb. Smart boy.

Mitchell studied the river.

The torrent swirled relentlessly, leaving an alarming question swimming in his mind.

How would the young boys survive the swift current?

THREE

Hazel held tightly to her son's jacket and tried hard to curtail the emotions threatening to explode. Jackson was now in the wilderness without a coat. She prayed he still had the warm sweater she'd packed for him. The mountain wilderness cooled at night, even in the summer season. *Lord, help me find the boys before nightfall.* Jackson was her everything, and she didn't know what she'd do if something happened to him.

Hazel struggled every day with being a single mom. When Garrison Neal found out she was pregnant, he'd left without as much as a goodbye. She'd had to pick up the broken pieces of her heart and move on—for her son's sake. At that point in her life, she hadn't given herself over to Christ and had made choices she wasn't proud of. Choices her father reminded her of constantly.

However, once Jackson was born, Frank Hoyt changed his tune and fell in love with his grandson. The child he nicknamed Bear Cub. Now the eight-year-old could do no wrong in his eyes.

It was only Hazel who could.

Her father had never forgiven her for selecting the university where she'd met Garrison. She'd fallen for him hard, fast. He'd enticed her with his good looks and impressive wallet. She wasn't raised to let money be her idol, but his rich parents had showed their love by gifts—and lots of them. So Garrison had learned by example and showered her with presents. Her college roommate had warned her about his sly ways, but she wouldn't listen. She got caught up in the whirlwind romance that eventually led her down a steep path. One that still shamed her today.

And one she refused to go down again.

After he left with no explanation, she'd learned through mutual friends that his parents had wanted the breakup. Hazel Hoyt was not of their social status and they'd threatened to disown Garrison, so he did the unthinkable and walked away from his child as if his relationship with Hazel had never happened.

Hazel had returned home with her proverbial tail tucked between her legs. Her mother had opened her arms wide, but her father had only given her a stern I-told-you-so lecture. Since that day, she'd given her life to Christ and raised her son with a deep faith in God.

Mitchell rested his hand on her shoulder. "You okay?"

His touch sent a tingle down her arm, but she ignored it. She would not succumb to attraction again. She'd vowed to remain single. "I have to get him back. He's my world." She stood too quickly and teetered.

Mitchell latched on to her, preventing a tumble. "You're still weak from your wound. Maybe you should go to the hospital. I can continue looking for Jackson and the boys."

Hazel wrenched herself free. "My son needs me. I'll be okay." She focused on the row of canoes tethered on a nearby rack and sucked in a breath.

"What is it?" Mitchell asked.

Her heart rate accelerated as she pointed a shaky finger to an empty slot. "They've taken a canoe."

He eyed the rack and then the river, his expression distorting. "Not good. Those rapids are running fast today."

"Wait." She counted. "All the other canoes are here." Hazel's chest tightened as a lump formed in her throat. "Five boys went in one boat? Jackson knows better."

"Has he canoed before?"

"Multiple times, but never on this river. My father forbids it, and for once, I agree with him." She bit her lip. "The boys must have been desperate to flee. Jackson would never have gone if that wasn't the case."

Mitchell untied a canoe. "Come on, they've had quite a head start. We need to get to them fast."

"Let me grab life jackets from the hut." *Lord, please let Jackson have done that.* Both Hazel and her father had taught the boy canoeing safety. She'd ingrained in his head never to go out on the water without some type of personal flotation device. Had he listened?

She scurried to the building and opened the door, holding her breath at what she'd find. She examined the area where the bright yellow life jackets were routinely stored and let out an elongated breath. The stack had been depleted, telling her Jackson had remembered the rule.

However, only one remained.

Not good.

She snatched it up and raced back outside. "Looks like the boys took life jackets." She raised the lifesaving device. "But there's only one left and the next shanty is ten kilometers from here."

"You take it. We don't have time to get others. We need to get moving." Mitchell grabbed paddles from the rack and thrust one toward her. "I'll be fine. Let's go."

Lord, keep us safe.

Hazel put the vest on and snatched the paddle, climbing into the canoe's bow.

Mitchell eased the watercraft into the river and hopped into the stern. He guided them toward the middle, and the current quickly whisked them downstream.

"I'm going to radio the team and give our location," Hazel yelled over her shoulder. "You okay with controlling the canoe?"

"I'm good."

Hazel pressed the button. "Shari, the boys have taken a canoe out on Whispering River. We're following. Current is swift today. Send the search party to different locations along the riverbank. Also, can you get a couple of student employees to come and get the horses? Take them back to the stables. We tethered them at the end of the trail." She gave them their current position.

"Copy that, Hazel," Shari said. "Stay safe. I'm praying for Jackson and those boys."

Their dispatch leader was like a second mother to Hazel and doted on Jackson.

"Appreciate it." Hazel clicked off and focused on the river in front of her.

A rumble of thunder sounded in the distance as fat raindrops splattered on the canoe.

Great, a storm on this swiftly running river did not mix well. Plus she hated storms ever since an accident almost claimed a friend on prom night when Hazel drove through the pelting rain. If only she had listened to her father when he told her the roads were too dangerous. The accident was her fault and created another wedge in their growing tumultuous relationship.

Their canoe hit a rapid and sprayed cold water in her face, stealing her breath and snapping her back to their situation. They needed all the prayers they could get right now. Her son's life depended on them. *Lord, please help.*

"Hazel, rock ahead."

She quickly swiped away the water, using the back of her hand, and firmed her grip on the paddle, rowing hard to get around a protruding boulder.

"That was close," Mitchell said. "If memory serves me correctly, we're coming up on more rapids. Let's hope they got off the river before. Check the forest. I'll keep the canoe straight."

Hazel removed her small binoculars from her vest pocket and observed both riverbanks, praying she'd catch a glimpse of the boys.

Unfortunately, only silence lived in the Micmore wilderness today.

"I don't see them." She averted her gaze back to the river. Mitchell required her undivided attention. She knew what lay ahead.

She dropped the binoculars and picked up her paddle just as the deadly rapids barreled them around a sharp bend.

Their canoe approached a fork in the river.

"Which way?" Mitchell yelled.

Lord, show me.

"Look. Over there." Mitchell pointed left.

She spied an object, and her breath hitched.

Jackson's superheroes pajama shirt hung on a fallen tree branch. Her son had left them another bread crumb.

However, Hazel knew what danger lay a couple of kilometers ahead.

Deadly sharp rocks hidden among turbulent rapids. A steep drop in the angry river.

She slumped forward in defeat as a question catapulted through her mind.

Had the boys survived the waterfall?

The canoe crashed into the rapids, throwing them upward, then back onto the water over and over like a cowboy riding a bull. Mitchell wrestled the small boat as waves of water splashed into his face, blocking his vision. His heartbeat thrashed in his ears with every bounce. "Hazel. Help me control the canoe."

She had frozen after seeing the pajama shirt. Obviously, she'd determined the boys had gone left toward the falls.

Not a good choice.

Thunder boomed as the rain transformed into sheets and pelted them sideways. Mitchell cleared water from his eyes and regained his paddle grip. "Hazel. Now!"

He hated to yell at her, but he needed her to snap out of whatever trance she'd fallen into.

She stiffened and thrust her paddle deeper into the water.

He steered them left toward the deadly waterfall.

Lord, my sister trusts You in all matters, so please... save those boys. Protect Hazel's son. And us too.

Fork lightning flashed, and seconds later, thunder boomed in response.

Mitchell gazed into the distance, examining the smoke on the Greenock Mountain Pass. The fires were getting closer and if lightning struck any trees, it would increase the blaze. He prayed the rain would smother the flames into a smoldering heap, so the unit crews could contain the situation.

He choked the paddle's handle until his hands ached. The thought of someone purposely setting fires made his blood boil. Firebug's foolishness had already taken innocent lives along with wildlife.

How long before they caught the man? What was his purpose in terrorizing the region?

Mitchell determined this was now personal. Hazel had been targeted, and for Bree's sake, he'd protect her and her son.

At all costs.

The canoe bounced around another corner and picked up speed, snapping his attention back to the river. The rapids were getting stronger, which meant they were closer to the waterfall.

Movement from the shoreline drew his attention.

Hairs prickled his neck and sent shivers crawling down his spine. Were they being followed?

"Hazel, the trees," he yelled over the thunderous rapids. "Someone's watching from the riverbank to your left. Stay alert."

She stopped paddling and rested her hand on her weapon, looking left. "Where? I don't see anyone."

He studied the forest, but other than the pounding rain and booming thunder, it remained in stillness. Whatever he'd seen—or assumed he'd seen—was gone.

"Must have been the rain." He steered them farther from the jagged rocks. Just to be safe. "Keep going. There's a clearing before the falls, right?"

She glanced over her shoulder. "Yes, I'm praying they got off the river there. There's a small old loggers' cabin nearby. A great place to hide."

But if they knew about the cabin, Firebug and whoever helped him probably did too.

His radio sputtered to life. "Boomer, update your status." His leader's stern voice crackled over the airways, telling Mitchell the man was not happy. Not that it surprised him. Carey Morgan did not like Mitchell and reminded him whenever the moment arose. The fact that the man's boss had appointed Mitchell unit crew leader against Morgan's wishes hadn't helped matters. Mitchell's determination to gain Morgan's trust spurred him on to excel in his role. One way to do that was to catch the Rocky Mountain Firebug.

Mitchell stopped paddling as they reached a short, rapids-free stretch and steered the canoe toward two fallen trees, wedging between them. He unhooked his radio. "Go ahead, Morgan."

"I understand you're shirking your duties and helping a park warden find kids. Get back to work and stop these fires." His strong, authoritative tone resonated over the sound of lingering rapids.

"Morgan, I'm in pursuit of Firebug. He's responsible for the attack on Warden Hoyt and we believe he orchestrated the abduction of a troop of young boys out camping. I catch Firebug and I stop the fires." Mitchell steered the canoe closer to the shore's edge.

"Oh, I know. I received a rather stern lecture from Supervisor Hoyt himself, complaining about you." He muttered to himself before continuing, "I don't appreciate hearing situation updates from that man. He's got a huge chip on his shoulder."

"Sorry, sir. I asked Smokey to update you. Obviously, our wires got crossed." He squeezed the radio tighter, his lips flattening. "Won't happen again."

"It better not, or Jacobs won't save your hide this time."

Division Supervisor Randy Jacobs had helped Mitchell with the vigorous wildland fire training, and when Mitchell came out top in his class, Randy had put him into the lead position of their unit. The man had been like an uncle to him throughout the years and had certainly helped, but Mitchell hoped his firefighting record also had something to do with getting the job.

"Morgan, we need to set up an EOC location somewhere in the park. I have a feeling Firebug isn't finished setting fires here." Thankfully, the wildfire units could coordinate and set up Emergency Operations Centers wherever required.

Hazel's radio crackled. "Hazel, come in."

Speaking of her father.

Mitchell addressed his leader. "Listen, I gotta run. I'm monitoring the fires from here. Don't worry. I'm in constant contact with Smokey." He gritted his teeth. Smokey had failed to give the boss an update. He'd definitely remind him to follow orders.

However, Mitchell sensed Smokey resented Mitchell having been chosen over him for the position.

"I've already called in the team to set up the EOC near the park's entrance. Keep me informed of any progress." Morgan clicked off.

Hazel dragged in her paddle. "Go ahead, Dad."

"Where are you?" Hoyt asked. "Why haven't I heard from you?"

Hazel huffed. "Kinda busy here, fighting rapids."

"Any sightings of Jackson?"

"None."

Hoyt muttered. "I need to tell you before you hear this from anyone else. The boys got separated. A park worker found two in a clearing, huddled under a tree."

Hazel peeked over her shoulder. "What? Are they okay? Did they give Jackson's location?"

"They're shaken up, but fine. They told us the other boys headed toward the river. I don't like it, Hazel."

Distress spread across her scrunched-up face. "Did the dogs catch a scent from his hat?"

"They did, close to your location, but then they lost it." Frank cleared his throat. "Find them before the storm gets worse and give me better updates. I'm counting on you."

"Copy that." Hazel sighed audibly.

Clearly, she didn't enjoy being ordered around either.

"We both don't need this hassle from our leaders,"

Mitchell said. "What we need is to find those boys. Let's keep going, but you remember what's ahead, right?"

"I know, but I have to find my son."

She would risk herself for those boys.

And he'd help her.

He nodded and pushed them from their position, guiding the canoe back into the rapids.

A gunshot sounded from the riverbank, and a bullet hit the hull.

Mitchell's muscles locked as terror threatened to overpower him. He tightened his grip on his paddles, scrambling to steady the canoe. His earlier assessment of someone lurking on the riverbank had been correct.

Hazel screamed and dived for cover, as she whipped out her gun.

Her rapid movement, coupled with the frothy rapids caused the canoe to tip. Mitchell fought to right it but failed. As they hit the next rise, they were thrown into the water.

Hazel's life jacket kept her buoyant, and she grasped a low-lying branch. It stopped her from being pulled into the upcoming rapids.

Mitchell struggled to keep his head above the water as the current swept him downstream. He flailed his arms.

"Mitchell!"

Hazel's garbled scream came as a large rapid crashed into him, immersing him before he could draw in a breath. One thought tumbled through his mind.

Would he survive the turbulent waters so he could help Hazel find her son and stop the Rocky Mountain Firebug?

FOUR

Hazel's grip on the tree limb slipped, and she plunged back into the rapids as her tightened chest sent her into panic mode. *Keep calm, Hazel. You've got this.* She must help Mitchell. It wouldn't be long before the current flushed him downstream toward the deadly waterfall. She had to act fast. Once again, she fumbled for another low-lying branch, but it was out of reach. So close but yet so far. "Come on," she yelled. She bounced farther along the riverbank and spied a larger, extended branch hanging over the water just ahead. This was her last window of opportunity before the river increased its nastiness and turned toward the drop. *Lord, help me!* As she approached her only means of safety, she reached high and grabbed the lifeline, holding on to it and hoisting herself upward. With her feet hanging, she shimmied along the branch toward the tree trunk. When she was safely over the shoreline, she dropped into the long weeds and sprang to her feet. She let out a breath and sprinted down the riverbank, watching for signs of Mitchell.

"Mitchell, where are you?" She inched closer to the edge, prepared to provide any type of aid she could give her childhood friend. The man who had stolen her heart all those years ago and shattered it in the same breath.

Focus, Hazel. You have more to think about than past silly crushes.

"Mitchell!" Hazel stumbled through the brush, following the river's flow and keeping an eye out for Bree's big brother.

As if in response to her cry, Mitchell's head burst out of the water, along with his flailing arms.

Hazel noticed rock formations downstream, close to his location. "Mitchell, try to grasp the rock. I'm coming!" She prayed he'd hear her over the thunderous rapids. The rain had picked up in intensity, obstructing her view. Hazel wiped the water from her face, clearing her vision, and hurried toward him.

She edged out onto the rock formations and prayed she wouldn't slip into the angry river. *Lord, I need to save him.*

A flash of lightning streaked across the sky, followed by a deafening thunderclap. She ignored the pounding in her head, pushed down the horror lurking inside, and pointed. "Grab the rock, Mitchell."

His body bounced toward them, and he reached out, grabbing the boulder's edge.

"Hold on! I'm coming." Hazel inched toward him and straddled the rock, anchoring herself. "Take my hand."

The fear in his widened eyes revealed the thoughts she guessed were tumbling through his mind. The possibility of drowning would catapult the strongest of men into distress.

"I've got you. Trust me." Would her words reassure him? After all, her small frame often planted doubts in her coworkers' minds. She'd seen it in their questioning eyes.

He nodded, and with his other hand, he grabbed on to hers.

Mustering strength and courage, she tugged upward.

Mitchell rested his head and chest on the surface, his breath exploding in rapid bursts. His feet still dangled in the raging current.

Hazel had to get him out before the river swallowed

him again. "You need to help me." She grasped his belt and, holding the back of his waistband, hauled him higher onto the boulder.

He shimmied forward until they were both safely on the rock. "Thank you. You saved my life." His words stumbled out in between strangled breaths.

"That was too close." Hazel surveyed the shoreline. "Did you see which way the shooter went?"

"Too busy fighting the rapids." He moved a wet strand of hair out of her eyes. "You okay?"

"I'll be fine once we rescue the boys." She refused to tell him how she really felt. Frustrated. Tired. Scared to death. She suppressed her thoughts and gestured toward the shoreline. "Let's get off these rocks." She pushed herself into a crouching position and walked over the formation back to solid ground.

Mitchell followed and sunk into the weeds. "Need to catch my breath. I forgot how hard it is to fight strong currents. Even carrying heavy firefighting equipment doesn't compare."

"Currents can pummel the strongest men's strength." Hazel plunked herself beside him and unhooked her radio, shaking the water off the device. "Our equipment is shot after that excursion. What do we do now?" She bit her lip to ward off the pending tears. Her son was still out there alone and now she was cut off from her team.

Mitchell squeezed her hand. "The team has our last coordinates. They will be out looking. Don't worry."

Hazel tore away from his grip and stood, holding her wounded side. "How can you say that? It's not that easy. Those boys are in danger, and now this storm is hampering everything."

What was she doing? She hated how harsh her words sounded. After all, he was out here risking his life to save Jackson and his troop. She hung her head. "I'm sorry,

Mitchell. You're only trying to encourage me. I never used to worry this much, but since Jackson was born, I struggle every day. Will kids at school like him? Will he hurt himself playing? Will he—"

"I get it, Hazel." Mitchell pushed himself upright. "You don't have to apologize. Your son means everything to you. Besides, isn't it a parent's job to worry?"

He smiled the lopsided grin that had always been her kryptonite.

Even after years of absence, her legs jellied whenever he looked at her with his signature smile and gorgeous green eyes.

Right now, in the vast wilderness, his closeness was her undoing. *Step away, Hazel. He only thinks of you as a little sister. Besides, you have a job to do. Find your son.*

She cleared her throat and walked deeper into the forest—and away from him. "I need to get my bearings." She looked left, then right. Seconds later, she snapped her fingers. "Wait, the old loggers' cabin isn't far from here." She pivoted and almost collided with Mitchell.

"Do you think they may have taken refuge there?" he asked.

"Maybe. Let's check it out." She didn't wait for his response, but walked ahead.

Five minutes later, Mitchell headed toward the high, dense bush close to the river. "I see something."

She pushed away low-lying branches and ducked, following him. Hazel stopped as she saw what he had spotted.

An abandoned canoe.

Hazel clasped her hand over her mouth. The boys had made it off the river. *Thank You, Lord.*

Mitchell squatted in front of the boat and brought out an object.

A whistle hanging from a short rope.

Her son had left another clue.

"That's Jackson's." She lifted her gaze upward. "Thank You, Lord."

Mitchell stood. "Your son is one smart boy. Not only did they survive a deadly river but he's leaving bread crumbs for us. You taught him well."

"My dad helped." She couldn't believe she was actually giving her stern father credit. However, he *had* been a tremendous help in conditioning Jackson to the outdoors and teaching him safety.

"I somehow think it was mostly your gentleness that shaped your son."

Hazel played with the cord bracelet her son had made. She never took it off. "You haven't met him." She kicked at the broken branch. "Let's head to the cabin. I'm guessing Jackson led the boys there." She dashed back through the trees and onto the path, not wanting him to see her reddened cheeks. She never could take a compliment well.

A shabby cabin came into view as they turned a bend. Sheltered in the thick woods, the small log structure had been in Micmore National Park for as long as Hazel could remember. According to her father, it had been inhabited by loggers hired to clear portions of the land years ago. After they finished the job, the place was abandoned and now she'd heard rumors of a man living in the forest and claiming the cabin as its only resident. However, no park workers had ever been able to catch him, leading most people to believe the vagrant didn't exist. Had someone fabricated the story? Hazel set aside the mysterious tale and marched toward the entrance. "Jackson! Are you in there?"

Mitchell pulled her back. "Be careful. We don't know how sturdy the cabin is or if anyone else is watching."

"Understood, but I need to know if they're here." She

clasped the railing and gingerly pressed her foot on the first step, testing its strength. It held.

"Let me go first." Mitchell shifted himself in front, making his way toward the rickety entrance.

Paint had all but peeled off the door, except for a small patch of reddish brown in the middle. The faded color matched the open window shutters. A full rain barrel sat at the end of the porch. Small flowerpots sprouting herbs were positioned on top of overturned pails. Maybe there was truth to the rumor that the vagrant had taken up residence in the park's cabin.

Mitchell eased open the door, but it stopped halfway. "It's stuck." He pushed harder and almost fell inward.

Hazel didn't miss Mitchell's gasp.

Something had alarmed the firefighter.

Lord, let it not to be—

She couldn't finish her unspoken prayer. She had to see for herself. Hazel held her breath and stepped inside. She waited for her eyes to adjust to the darkened room as she struggled to contain the terror wanting to consume her body over what they'd find. For her son's sake, she had to press forward. But something stopped her in her tracks.

A body lay blocking the door's path, a knife thrust deep into his chest, and blood pooled on the decrepit floor. The man's head faced the opposite direction from where they stood.

Had this been the work of the Rocky Mountain Firebug?

Mitchell yanked Hazel away from the body. He knew enough from his police officer buddy, Zac Turner, that they couldn't contaminate the scene, and from her bewildered, widened eyes, he guessed she was in some sort of shock. Not that he blamed her. Finding a dead man would do that to the strongest individual. He rubbed her arm. "You going to be okay?"

She jerked from his touch. Her gaze shifted around the one-room cabin and stopped at the fireplace. "The boys aren't here?"

He followed her eye movement. The smell of smoke lingered in the small enclosure, revealing a recent fire. "Doesn't look like it." He turned back to the body and squatted. Dressed in a park uniform and an orange vest, the victim looked to be in his mid-to-late fifties, based on his salt-and-pepper-streaked hair. "Do you recognize him?" Mitchell asked as he checked for a pulse.

Hazel walked around the body and observed the man's face. Her hand flew to her mouth. "Yes, that's one of our maintenance workers, Stan Cahall. Is he—"

"He's gone."

"Oh man. He was such a nice person. Kind, gentle." Her voice broke, revealing her sadness over Stan's death.

"I'm guessing from his vest, he probably joined the search team."

"He did. I saw him earlier. There's no way he wouldn't have tried to find those boys. He loves…loved kids." Hazel swatted a tear from her face and cleared her throat.

"I'm sorry for your loss. I can tell you cared for him." Mitchell pushed himself to his feet and walked around the body, searching without touching. Stan wore a belt, but the radio holster was empty. "I don't see his two-way. Look through the cabin but don't touch anything. Perhaps he dropped it. We need to get the police here."

Mitchell carefully moved around the room, searching for Stan's radio, but came up empty. He dug his nails into his palms, frustration settling into his bones. How could they call for help? Where was Hazel and Bree's God now, when they needed Him the most?

That was a question he had wanted answers to for a long time. For now, he'd have to wait. They had to find the boys. "Can you think of another place Jackson might hide?"

Hazel scratched her head and paced, staying clear of the body. "Not in this part of the park."

Mitchell gestured toward the items strewn about the cabin. A sleeping bag lay crumpled in a corner, a stack of torn magazines beside it. Discarded food containers were piled on the coffee table. "Hazel, do you think the park vagrant is living here? These items tell me it's a possibility."

Her eyes widened. "You don't think he killed Stan, do you?"

"What do you know about him?"

"Just that different campers have seen him rummaging through their tents and garbage cans. Our park workers have spotted him occasionally, but somehow he always disappears." She nudged the magazines with her foot. "We've had no reports of him being hostile. I can't imagine he did this."

"I agree, especially when he hasn't been aggressive. I wonder what his story is."

"No one seems to know." She stopped pacing and pointed at Stan's hand. "Wait, what's he holding?"

Mitchell squatted and gingerly shifted Stan's arm, revealing the object in question.

A tiny candle protruded from the man's hand. How had Mitchell missed that before?

Hazel let out a cry. "Firebug killed Stan. The candle is his signature." She plunked onto a tattered couch and buried her head in her hands.

Mitchell sat beside her and wrapped one arm around her shoulders, bringing her close. "You don't know that for sure. He could have been lighting a candle simply for light." Somehow Mitchell doubted his own words.

She straightened. "Firebug starts fires using candles."

"Why do you think Stan was here?"

"Maybe after I radioed Dad to tell them Jackson left his jacket at the river, Stan guessed the boys would head to the cabin."

Something caught Mitchell's eye. He walked to the rusty sink and dilapidated counter in the corner of the room. Wadded granola bar wrappers sat discarded next to an empty water bottle. "Did you pack chocolate chip granola bars with Jackson?"

She stood. "Yes, why?"

He pointed to the wrappers. "Looks like the boys were here."

"Stan may have found the kids, started a fire to warm them up, and was getting ready to take them back to the station when Firebug interrupted them." Hazel grabbed Mitchell's arm. "He has my boy!"

He brought her into his arms and let her sob on his shoulder. Her lavender scent intermingled with river smells and wafted into his nose, along with a thought. She fit perfectly in his embrace. The little sister-like girl that followed him around like a lost puppy had grown into a woman of beauty. *Why are you thinking these thoughts at a time like this?* He chewed the inside of his mouth to ward off his growing infatuation. "Stan may have fought him off so the boys could escape. Or maybe the vagrant helped. We can't jump to conclusions." However, his mind formulated what seemed a million scenarios. No matter what had happened, he hoped the boys got away from Firebug's clutches. Still, one question remained.

Why did he want them so badly?

There had to be a significant reason he would risk getting caught and go to the trouble of chasing boys through the park in a thunderstorm.

"Why do you think Firebug wanted the troop?" he asked.

She sniffed and freed herself from his hold. "No idea. Aaron was killed before he could tell us more."

"Perhaps they saw his face?"

"Possibly." She paused. "We need the storm to subside. We have to find the boys."

"Agreed. Plus, hopefully, we'll run into the search party and be able to call in the police."

Hazel approached Stan's body again and squatted. "I'm so sorry you died trying to save my boy. You were a good man, Stan Cahall."

"Was he married?"

"Widower. Macy died a year ago from breast cancer." She bowed her head.

Was she praying over him? "Hazel, we need—" The smell of kerosene bushwhacked his nose. "Do you smell that?"

"No, what?"

Scraping sounded outside the door along the small porch, followed by hammering. Seconds later, the shutters slammed shut and boards sliding into place rattled the window. Darkness shadowed the tiny cabin.

Chills iced his spine.

Someone was sealing them inside. Why?

Hazel sprang upright. "Who's out there?"

He sprinted to the door and pushed.

It wouldn't budge.

A whoosh resonated.

He'd recognize that sound anywhere.

The assailant had set a fire at the entrance. It was only a matter of time before it consumed the run-down cabin.

Mitchell turned and inspected the room from the little light that shone through cracks in the tattered walls.

No way out. They were trapped in their fiery tomb.

FIVE

Flames assaulted the door and spread to the log walls. The intense heat pushed Hazel backward and she stumbled over Stan, falling to the floor with a thump. Her heart's rhythm matched the pounding in her head as terror consumed her body. *God, where are You? Save us!* She scrambled to her feet. "Why are the flames moving so quickly in this storm?"

"He sprayed the outside with kerosene. That's what I smelled." Mitchell hurried to each wall, fingering the surface.

"What are you doing?"

"Checking to see if all the walls are hot." He shuffled to the rear of the cabin.

"How will we get out? There's no back door." Once again, tears threatened to fall. How many times had her emotions caught her off guard today? Her father had taught his children to keep their feelings to themselves. *Never let anyone see you falling apart. It shows you're weak, and a Hoyt is far from it.*

How could she not when her son's life was on the line? Would she ever see him again? Would she die here in this cabin?

Questions consumed her mind, and she fought to remain in control. She inhaled to calm herself, but smoke cut her breath short, stealing her air and her resolve to stay strong. She sank to the ground and coughed.

Mitchell kneeled beside her. "I know this is hard, but we have to find an escape route. Stay low and help me look for weaknesses in the back wall. We might get out that way. Can you do that?"

Her lip trembled. "I don't know." Her father would be so ashamed of her right now.

He squeezed her shoulder. "You can, Hazel. For Jackson's sake."

She tensed. He was right. She could.

Hazel pushed aside thoughts of her father and focused on something her mom always said when her children required encouragement.

Whenever your strength is gone, look to your Father. The One who holds you in the palm of His hands. He'll provide endurance. Trust Him. Trust in yourself.

Hazel nodded, willed stamina into her body and crawled to the wall.

"Good girl." Mitchell positioned himself at the opposite end. "Let's do this together and quickly."

They each inspected the surface, feeling for any type of vulnerabilities. Hazel's fingers stopped when she hit a protruding nail. She pushed inward and the rotted log crumbled away. "Here, Mitchell!"

He rushed to her side.

Together they broke apart the wood, creating a hole.

Smoke permeated the room, continuing to steal their precious oxygen.

Hazel breathed in air from the hole to gain momentum and pushed harder to break the wood.

Flames erupted behind them. The fire had breached the front wall and now raged inside the cabin.

Mitchell coughed. "We need to work faster. Let's push with our feet. Lean back and kick. Together."

She balanced on her backside, holding her feet in place, and waited for his cue.

He matched her position. "Go!"

Together, they kicked at the planks over and over until more broke free. Air swooshed inside and Hazel breathed in.

"That's good," Mitchell said. "Quick, get out."

She wormed her way through the hole and exited into the forest. Rain still hampered the area, and she prayed it would smother the flames, stopping its spread. They needed a win.

Mitchell struggled to get through the small space, but after a few tries, he wiggled out. He ran to her side. "You okay?"

She nodded and breathed in more air, exhaling slowly to calm her rapid heartbeat. They were safe.

For now.

"How can we stop the fire? We can't let it spread." She leaned against a Douglas fir.

Mitchell rubbed his brow. "I remember seeing a rain barrel on the porch as well as pails. That will help. I hope we can get to them. They're close to the entrance. Thankfully, the rain is helping contain it somewhat."

Hazel popped upright. "Wait. Do you think whoever blocked us in is gone?"

"I'll check out front. You stay here." He didn't wait for her reply and bounded through the forest, stopping behind different trees, obviously using caution before moving out into the open.

Lord, thank You for Mitchell. His quick thinking about looking for structure damage saved our lives.

Her respect meter for the man raised a notch. Even though he had hurt her all those years ago, she'd already seen how he'd matured into a man of integrity.

And a man she'd like to get to know more.

Her jaw dropped. Where had the thought come from? *Hazel, remember how Garrison stomped all over your heart.* She wouldn't risk it getting broken again. Plus she had to think of her son.

Seal up the fortress around your heart and throw away the key.

But how could she do that with the strong, handsome firefighter back in the picture? It was easy when he was out-of-sight-out-of-mind. But now? Her childhood crush bull-rushed her and a question emerged.

Bree, why didn't you tell me he was home?

Was there a story there? Her best friend had been away on a mission trip for the last few months. Perhaps she wasn't aware Mitchell had returned. Hazel would be sure to ask Bree when she arrived home later today.

Maybe by then Hazel would be at home snuggled up, with Jackson by her side. One could always hope.

Mitchell sprinted around the corner, beckoning her to the front.

Time to set aside thoughts of relationships and handsome firefighters. They must stop the spread of this fire and get back to searching for her son.

Those boys were counting on her, and she wouldn't disappoint them.

Even if it meant sacrificing herself to get them to safety.

Mitchell examined the smoldering cabin to ensure no new flames had erupted. He couldn't have it spreading into the wilderness or they'd have another problem to deal with besides finding the missing boys. Thankfully, the rain and the water from the barrel had helped them in their effort to extinguish the blaze. He studied Hazel. Her soot-covered, scrunched face revealed her dwindling stamina. It was only a matter of time before her adrenaline depleted and she broke down. Mitchell rolled his shoulders, determination setting in. When that happened, he would be there for her.

Every step of the way.

He hadn't realized how much guilt he'd carried around over leaving her dateless for her prom. Bree hadn't told him the full story. Not that it surprised him. Their relationship over the past few years had been strained, ever since he'd introduced her to Ivy. Bree had instantly sensed something wrong in his girlfriend's character and Mitchell wouldn't listen to his sister. If only he had, he never would've endured Ivy's sinister and obsessed personality. A restraining order hadn't stopped the woman from kidnapping him and burying him alive. Thankfully, she'd missed his cell phone stashed inside his inner jacket pocket, which had saved his life. Zac's team was able to ping his last known location at the gravesite before Ivy had buried Mitchell.

He realized then his spidey senses were skewed when it came to reading women. He promised himself he'd never be caught unaware again, and the only way to do that was to remain single. However, being around Hazel today had chipped away at his resolve, but the questions remained...

Could he trust this woman? Or would she deceive him like Ivy?

So far today, Hazel's stamina, determination and bravery had impressed him. She'd saved his life back in the river. No, she wasn't like Ivy. Not at all.

Hazel brushed ashes off her soiled park uniform and eyed her watch. "Are we ready? It's now six thirty. I need to keep searching before it gets dark."

His stomach growled, reminding him he hadn't eaten all day and any food they'd stuffed into their backpacks had fallen into the river when their canoe tipped. However, he'd survive. He had to, for Hazel's sake. "Yes. The rain will help keep any smoldering embers from reigniting." He looked left, then right. "Which way would the boys have gone?"

She placed her hands on her hips, peering in both directions. "I believe Jackson would follow the river's flow."

Mitchell spied a long broken branch and scooped it up. "Keep your eyes peeled for anyone following us." He white-knuckled the walking stick. Not that it would help against bullets or knives, but it gave him a bit of comfort to have some type of weapon in his hands. "Let's head out."

Two hours later, Mitchell and Hazel came to a fork in the path. Their exhaustive search had yielded no results. Wherever the boys had gone, Jackson hadn't provided any more bread crumbs, leading Mitchell to believe the suspect had taken them somewhere and kept them hidden. Mitchell wouldn't voice his theory, as he didn't want to further dampen Hazel's mood. She had clammed up an hour into their hunt and her sagging shoulders revealed her agony.

Mitchell stopped and looked left, then right. "Where does this trail lead? It's been years since I've been on this side of the park."

She pointed left. "That leads to Whispering Ridge. The other way takes us back toward the walk bridge over Whispering River and to our park station."

"Which way do you want to go?" Mitchell leaned on his stick, willing strength into his limbs. His weary bones told him he required both rest and nourishment, but he wanted Hazel to make the call. "It's getting dark—"

Movement to his right caught his attention and interrupted his statement. Someone approached and until Mitchell knew if it was friend or foe, they'd stay hidden. He nudged Hazel behind a tree and held his breath.

Voices grew louder as footfalls shuffled on the rocky

path. "We have to find Boomer," a voice said. "They're predicting this storm is going to get bad."

"That's Kane." Mitchell shuffled out onto the trail. "Smokey! We're over here."

"Boomer!" Smokey hustled toward him. "Where have you been? We've been trying to contact you."

"I'm afraid both of our radios are waterlogged from our spill into Whispering River." Mitchell noticed the other male beside his coworker. "Good to see you again, Levi."

Smokey slapped Levi's back. "He joined the search for the boys."

"Glad to help." Levi handed Mitchell a radio. "To replace your other one."

"Thanks." Mitchell gestured toward Hazel. "Have you two met Hazel Hoyt?"

"Not had the pleasure. I think I'd remember her beautiful face. I'm Kane Everson, wildland firefighter extraordinaire. This is Levi Dotson, our unit's communication specialist." Smokey stuck out his hand. "Heard lots about you and the Hoyt family. Sorry about your boy."

Hazel shook both men's hands. "Thanks. Listen, can you contact the police? They need to send a team to the old log cabin along Whispering River. We found our park's maintenance worker, Stan Cahall, dead. Stabbed."

"Plus we had to put out a fire at the cabin, so there will be extensive damage," Mitchell said.

Smokey's eyes widened. "I'm on it."

"I really appreciate your help in the search, guys. Have you spotted any sign of the boys?" Hazel wiped her brow, smudging soot.

Lightning flashed, illuminating the darkened clouds. A deafening thunderclap followed. Not good.

Hazel startled and inched closer to Mitchell.

Or did he imagine her movement?

Perhaps it was time to take shelter, but how would he convince her to, with her son still lost in the wilderness?

A chill slithered through Hazel's body as the evening temperatures dropped. The relentless storm once again threatened the area—and the boys. *Lord, where are they? Show me! I need my son to be safe.* Hazel had been pleading with God all day, but He hadn't responded. Jackson was still out there and the fact that he hadn't left any more clues terrified Hazel. Did that mean Firebug had found the boys and captured them?

No, she couldn't think that way.

She rubbed her arms to warm the chill settling into her bones. The rain and river had soaked her, and even after drying off, the coolness had remained. She pictured her plush, multicolored plaid comforter on her bed. How she longed to be snuggled under it with Jackson, reading his favorite adventure book.

"Hazel, did you hear me?" Mitchell squeezed her arm.

She snapped to attention, his touch sending a jolt fluttering across her skin. "What?"

Mitchell's green eyes widened. "Smokey said they're calling for this storm to intensify. It's not safe to stay out here."

She jerked her arm away. "I'm not leaving until we find Jackson."

Mitchell looked at his watch. "Smokey, you and Levi head back. We'll keep searching for now. Radio us if you find out anything else."

"Boomer, they're calling off the search because of the bad weather and late hour," Kane said. "Morgan ordered you back in. He's waiting for your report."

Hazel shook her head. "We still have time to search."

Kane withdrew two granola bars and water bottles, handing them to Mitchell and Hazel. "I won't convince you otherwise, so at least eat something." He turned to Levi. "You have extra flashlights?"

The tall, dark-haired man with the mustache and goatee nodded, removing a couple from his backpack. "Be careful. Dangerous wildlife lurk in this wilderness."

Like I don't already know that, but thanks for pointing it out. Ouch. She was getting testy in her weary state. She smiled and took the flashlight. "Thanks for this."

"Smokey, I have a question." Mitchell stuffed his light into his pocket and unwrapped the granola bar. "Why didn't you inform Morgan I was helping Hazel search for the boys?"

Kane raked his hand through his shoulder-length hair. "I got busy setting up the EOC and totally forgot."

"He reamed me out."

"Sorry, dude."

The man's voice sounded sincere, but Hazel didn't miss the look of anger flash on his face before it disappeared. Was there a territory fight happening between these two?

She set the thought aside and pointed ahead. "Mitchell, let's head toward Whispering Ridge before it gets too dark."

"And before the rain intensifies." Levi clucked his tongue. "You do not want to be up there when that happens."

"Thanks, guys, for the equipment," Mitchell said. "Tell Morgan and Frank Hoyt we're heading back soon. Got that, Smokey?"

Kane saluted. "Your funeral, dude. You know Morgan's temper." He pivoted and marched back down the trail.

Levi tagged behind his coworker.

More thunder rumbled, matching their foul moods.

Hazel flipped the light on. "That was harsh. What's going on with you two?" She walked toward the ridge, ignoring the rain battering the trees.

Mitchell followed. "No idea. For some reason, Smokey has had it in for me after I was appointed as unit crew leader."

"Maybe he resents the fact you got it over him."

"Possibly. We went to high school together, but back then, we always got along." He paused. "Well, at least I thought we did."

"Tell me, why did you switch from a structure to a wildland firefighter?" She shone her light into the trees, searching for signs of the boys. "Isn't your current job seasonal?"

"It is, but I have a meeting with the Bowhead Springs fire chief in a couple of weeks to talk about helping at their station in the off-season. As for taking the unit crew position, my first love is the mountains and wilderness. Plus I wanted to be back home. I've missed Alberta. Let's head farther into the trail."

An hour later, Mitchell stopped walking and stooped to the ground. "What do we have here?"

Hazel ignored another jab of pain and bent low to check out Mitchell's discovery, steadying herself on her heels.

A jacket was stuffed into the crevice between two rocks at the fork in the trail. A tree limb sheltered it from the rainstorm. Someone had definitely planted the coat there on purpose. Another bread crumb.

Jackson.

Hazel leaned closer and sucked in a breath.

An arrow drawn in dark red beside the jacket pointed toward Whispering Ridge, giving searchers the direction to follow.

"Is that—" Hazel stopped. She couldn't finish her question. Her heart palpitated as terror consumed her body. She lost her balance and fell backward.

Lord, make this not be Jackson's blood.

SIX

Mitchell shone the light closer and examined the mark's source of ink. He rubbed the roughly sketched arrow with his finger. Instantly it smudged, revealing its freshness. He smelled his finger and a metallic odor filled his nose. No! His pulse pounded in his ears. There was no doubt in his mind. Someone had used blood to leave the clue, but the question remained. Was it Jackson's?

"It's blood, isn't it?" Hazel grabbed his arm. "Tell me."

"I'm sorry. It is, but let's not go there yet."

"It has to be Jackson, leaving another crumb." Hazel sobbed. "My boy is hurt and away from his mama."

"Maybe not." Another thought entered his mind. What if it wasn't Jackson but their captors drawing anyone who followed into a trap? They had to think this new clue through completely before taking off in the arrow's direction.

"It's. The. Only. Answer." Hazel's words came in between sobs.

"Hazel, what if it's a trick? Someone leading us down a wrong path?"

Her face twisted into obvious pain. Pain from the possibility her son was wounded and she couldn't do anything about it.

"That's not what my broken heart is telling me. Mothers

have a sense about their children." A tear rolled down her cheek, and she dropped to the ground. "He's in trouble."

Mitchell gathered her into an embrace and rested his chin on her head. He stayed silent and rocked her, letting her cry. What words of comfort could he offer? Words were not his forte but his mother's. *Mom, what would you say to someone in this situation?* He wished he could ask, but his mom had died from a heart attack last year. Her absence from their lives only personified the wedge growing between him and Bree. His father had passed away from cancer when they were teenagers. Bree and Mitchell were the only Booths left.

A saying his mom had coined filtered into his thoughts. *When you don't know what to say, be silent. Just be present. Listen and pray for guidance.*

He hadn't prayed much lately, so he'd adhere to the rest of his mother's advice and be present. Right now, silence was the only prayer he'd give.

Thunder boomed around them as fresh raindrops hammered the forest. Mitchell inched them closer under the tree's shelter. Darkness blanketed them, bringing another wave of trepidation into the wilderness.

Calling off the search had been the right decision. The storm and nightfall would disrupt any further rescue attempts. There were too many slippery paths on the edge of the mountainous region. Mitchell had to get Hazel back home, but would she agree and leave her son behind?

"I need to find those boys." Hazel pushed herself back as if reading his thoughts and wiped her eyes before standing. Seconds later, she grabbed her side and doubled over.

"Hazel, let me see your wound." He stood and eyed her side. Fresh blood had soaked her shirt. "You're bleeding again. We need to have someone treat you properly."

"But, Jackson—"

"You're in no condition to continue. Please, for the boys' sake. I can tell you've been fighting your weakening condition all day. You need rest." Would she concede? He remembered her stubborn attitude from the times she'd spent with his sister.

She let out a breath, seething through her teeth. "Fine, but we're back out here at daybreak."

"I promise." He saluted. "Scout's honor."

His radio crackled. "Boomer, I'm here with Supervisor Hoyt. Give us a report," his boss's angry voice blasted.

Mitchell unhooked his radio. "We're close to Whispering Ridge. We have reason to believe the boys went in that direction."

"The storm is intensifying. You need to return to base. Now." The man meant business. "Plus I need your incident report. You should have come back when I said so. You're proving to me you can't follow orders very well. Not a good start to your role here. I don't care if you're good friends with our supervisor. If you continually disobey me, I'll be forced to replace you. Do you hear me?"

Mitchell resisted the urge to throw the radio against a tree. Instead, he rubbed the bridge of his nose and counted to five in his head. "Those boys are still out here. But I think Hazel is—"

A commotion sailed through the airwaves. "Hazel, are you trying to get yourself killed? You need to come home." Frank Hoyt's authoritative voice echoed through the rain-soaked forest. "That ridge is dangerous at the best of times, let alone in a pounding storm."

Hazel snatched the radio from Mitchell. "Dad, I'm not leaving my son and those boys out here alone." Her tone conveyed her determination.

Oh boy. So much for her earlier decision.

Frank mumbled. "Hazel, it kills me not to go out there

and continue searching for my Bear Cub, but we've pulled everyone out of the wilderness. You know what the mountainous region is like with all those trails and cliffs. It's too dangerous. They're predicting this storm is getting worse with the possibility of multiple lightning strikes."

"All the more reason to find those boys!" Hazel screamed.

Mitchell placed his hand on her shoulder. He must calm her sudden switch in mood or she'd make rash decisions and that could prove deadly.

"You're tired and need rest and nourishment. You're not doing them any good in your condition. Hazel, you might get hurt," Frank huffed. "Besides, I taught Jackson how to survive in the wilderness. He's smart, even at his young age. Micmore is full of caves. I bet that's where they are right now."

"But we just found blood, Dad."

Silence shot through the radio.

"Where?" Frank asked.

Hazel turned to face the rock. "At the fork in the trail leading toward the ridge. Someone drew an arrow using blood. We're guessing it was Jackson giving us a clue to their direction. He could be hurt. I need to get to him."

"Daughter, this is not the answer."

"Sorry, but it is. I'll be back soon with my son." Hazel switched off the radio and handed it to Mitchell. "Changed my mind. You can return to camp or come with me. Your choice."

She marched in the direction of the blood-drawn arrow, leaving him with a debate raging in his mind.

Which was worse? Facing his angry boss or a mama bear trying to find her cub?

Mitchell suppressed a sigh and followed mama bear.

He would not leave her alone. Not in her hour of need nor in a dangerous wilderness.

* * *

Another jab of pain sliced through Hazel's side, and she winced but kept walking as determination to find her son overpowered her. She'd almost given up…until her father demanded she come home. How dare he order her around. She was a grown woman capable of both defending herself and protecting her son. The throbbing from her wound told her otherwise, but she'd fight through the pain. Her son's life was more important than a simple ache. She pressed her hand firmly over the injury and shone the flashlight through the wilderness. "Jackson! Where are you?" Yelling probably wasn't the best option when hiding from assailants, but she must try.

Mitchell fell into step with her. "So much for your earlier decision."

"Frank Hoyt doesn't tell me what to do when it comes to my son." She shone the beam on the path's other side. "You can go if you want."

"And leave you by yourself? In the forest with a wound that is clearly worse than you let on earlier? No way." He halted. "Besides, I'd never hear the end of it from both your father and Morgan. No, you made that decision for us."

Even in the fading daylight, Hazel didn't miss the scowl on Mitchell's handsome face. He was angry, and how could she blame him? It wasn't enough she was putting her own life on the line, but his too? *Hazel, you know better. Dad's right. This wilderness is dangerous at the best of times and these are not the best of times.*

She stopped walking. "I'm sorry. You're right. I should have talked to you before telling my father I was staying. He just makes me so angry, and I lost it. I've never been the best at controlling my temper when I'm around him, but Jackson must be so scared and alone. The idea of leaving him tore at this mama's heart." She touched her side as another pain hit and her fingers felt wet. She was bleeding again…or was it *still*? Her adrenaline dissipated and her weakened limbs screamed for her to concede. But how could she admit that now, when Mitchell was willing to sacrifice himself and stay with her? She placed her bloody hand behind her back, out of sight. "Can we move on while we have a smidgen of daylight?"

He pursed his lips and waved his hand toward the path. "Let's go."

An hour later, under total cover of darkness, Hazel rested on a rock sheltered by a tree. The relentless rain had soaked them and the increasing pain from her side was stealing her strength. Defeat hit her hard and she struggled to contain her emotions.

They'd failed to find the boys or any further clues as to their whereabouts. The boys had not taken refuge in any caves in the area. The higher she and Mitchell went, the more they risked slipping off the path. It had turned ugly and their search would only take them closer to the deadly cliffs.

Had Jackson led the boys up there? If so, it wouldn't have been by choice. They had either gotten lost or they'd been forced by gunpoint.

And that thought scared her to the core.

Lord, I don't understand. Why haven't You shown me where they are?

Mitchell sat beside her and nudged her leg. "What are you thinking?"

His compassionate tone revealed the kindness she remembered from years ago. His closeness played on her emotions, sending her heart's rhythm into overdrive.

Dare she share her true thoughts? He'd only just come back into her life today. He hadn't wanted to talk about

God earlier, so would her doubts tear him further from his faith?

She looked away, biting her lip. "I'm scared you'll judge me as a hypocrite."

He squeezed her hand. "Never."

"I just don't understand why God isn't showing me where my son is after I've pleaded with Him all day."

"I'm no expert on God, but I remember my mom saying once that sometimes we may not understand His silence, but He will answer. In His timing."

She let out a staggered breath. "But what if I don't like the answer?"

"Then He will give you the strength to endure the storm." His pregnant pause thundered in the forest. "At least, that's what my mom told me."

Was it really that simple? Hazel had been through so much in her life and she thought she knew God well. She grew up going to church with her siblings and mother, but had strayed during college. Something she'd always regretted. But God gave her a gift through it all—Jackson—a second chance. After giving birth, she had totally surrendered to Christ and placed her trust in Him. She'd done all the right things. Gone to church, studied His word, prayed…everything. But Jackson's disappearance today rocked her faith through and through. She was a failure and a fraud. Would God still love her for her doubts? For not being a steadfast daughter of the King?

She dug her nails deep into her wet palms. Time to move on. Thoughts of God could wait. A pang of guilt jabbed her heart. "Where should we look next?"

Mitchell pushed himself into a standing position and wiped the raindrops from his forehead. "I'm a little leery about going higher on the ridge in this weather, Hazel. Don't you think it's time to head back?"

Was he right? Her weary body told her she wasn't doing her son any good, especially if she passed out from exhaustion, but her heart screamed for her to keep going. "Another half hour and we'll head back. I promise."

Lightning flashed and revealed a figure in the distance, pointing a gun in their direction.

Piercing pain stabbed her side, robbing her of words and silencing any hope of warning Mitchell. Dots flickered as a curtain of darkness closed slowly over her vision.

A shot rang out moments before Hazel's legs buckled and she dropped into blackness, leaving her with one thought.

I've failed my son and Mitchell.

SEVEN

Rain splatted on Mitchell's face, jarring him awake as questions zinged through his brain. What happened? Where was he? Why did his side— The shot. He recalled the blast of the gunshot and now his left side felt as if it were on fire. "Hazel!" He struggled to sit, but searing pain forced him back down.

Hazel lay unconscious beside him. She'd fainted just as gunfire echoed in the forest. He had tried to stop her fall, but the pain sent him into darkness. How long had he been out and where was the assailant? He slowly eased himself up and listened for movement, but only silence greeted him.

The attack confirmed one thing to Mitchell. The blood arrow had indeed been a trap, luring them deeper into the forest so the Rocky Mountain Firebug could kill them. Their deaths would stop their pursuit and allow him to further his mission.

Whatever that was.

Mitchell struggled to move closer to Hazel. *Lord, I know I haven't prayed in, like...years...but will You help me? Not for my sake, but Hazel's. I need to get her to safety.*

He shifted his position and unhooked his radio, praying his fall hadn't broken it. Mitchell hit the button. "Micmore Crew, need help. SOS." His words came out garbled and weak. He cleared his throat and took a breath. "Boomer requesting assistance. Anyone out there?"

Silence.

Were they too far up the mountain ridge?

He tried again. "Anyone?"

"Boomer, this is Levi."

Mitchell struggled to clear his foggy brain and focus. He breathed in. "Levi, I've been shot and Hazel is unconscious. Need help."

"You're wounded? Let me grab Smokey." A ruckus sounded in the background.

"Boomer, where are you?" Smokey asked.

Mitchell rubbed his throbbing head and tried to recollect how far they'd hiked from the fork in the path. The rain and storms had slowed their progress, but exactly how much distance had they'd traveled? *Think, Mitch.*

He pushed the radio button. "We're approximately three kilometers north of the fork on the Whispering Ridge Trail. Send medical help, but be aware. Assailants are armed and dangerous."

"Understood. ETA delayed because of this weather. Take cover." Smokey's curse sailed through the radio. "You should have come back before the storm worsened. Morgan told you to."

Mitchell clenched his jaw as pain jabbed his side. "Smokey, I don't need a lecture right now. I need help." His raised voice sounded over the rain splattering in the forest.

Hazel stirred beside him.

A coyote howled nearby, and Mitchell cringed. Not only did he need to keep them safe from assailants but from wildlife.

Mitchell mustered strength and sat upright. He had to find shelter. "Listen, there's a cave a couple kilometers from the fork in the trail. I'll get us there. Somehow."

"Sending paramedics and police," Smokey said.

"Copy that." Mitchell shoved the radio back into his belt and dragged himself closer to Hazel. "Wake up."

She groaned and shifted.

"We need to move." Mitchell shook her again. "We've been compromised. Can you sit?"

Hazel hoisted herself onto her elbows. "Yes."

"Take it slow." He tugged gently on her arm, helping her sit up. "You fainted just before someone shot at us."

"I remember. I turned and saw a figure in the trees raise a gun, but before I could say anything, a powerful pain incapacitated me. Then I felt myself falling. You okay?"

"I got shot, but I'm pretty sure the bullet only grazed me. However, it hurts like the dickens." Mitchell pressed on his side. "I've called for help, but we need to get to the cave down the trail. We're sitting ducks here."

Coyotes howled again as if warning them to leave their territory or pay the price.

"See what I mean? I heard them earlier." Mitchell pressed harder on his side. He was losing blood.

"Lord, please protect the boys from the wildlife," Hazel whispered.

"I have to believe the boys are somewhere safe. I suspect Firebug used the arrow to lure us here and kill us."

"But why not ensure we're dead?"

"Maybe the coyotes scared them off."

Hazel stood up and positioned her hands under his arms. "Can you stand?"

He nodded and leaned toward her, allowing her to pull him up. "I'm supposed to be the one helping you."

She huffed. "I'm hardly a damsel in distress. I'm a Hoyt, remember? My father didn't raise any of us girls to be wussies."

"No doubt." Pain assaulted him and he bit down hard

on the inside of his mouth, curbing an audible wince. He had to stay strong for Hazel. For the boys. For all of them. *You can do this.* "Let's go."

An hour later, after lots of breaks, Mitchell entered a cave and shone his flashlight, inspecting the damp hideout for any animals taking shelter from the storm. Thankfully, the area was free of bears or any other critters. "We're good."

They positioned themselves on a boulder, and Mitchell set the flashlight down to brighten the cave. The beam rested on Hazel. She'd closed her eyes, but her staggered breathing told him she wouldn't be able to take much more either.

They both required medical assistance and lots of rest.

Mitchell reached over and grabbed her hand. "Help will be here soon."

Her bottom lip quivered, and she opened her eyes. "I should have listened to you earlier and returned to the ranch. It's my fault you got shot."

"Let's get one thing straight right now. I'm a big boy and I make my own decisions." He shifted the light's beam onto the ground, but not before he caught her beautiful hazel eyes widening. Eyes he could get lost in if he allowed himself to. *Focus.* "This is not your fault. It's Firebug's."

"For once, I should have listened to Dad. Sometimes I'm too stubborn."

Mitchell chuckled. "Well, I'm not going to argue. I remember your feistiness from your constant squabbles with Bree."

"Speaking of Bree, why didn't she tell me you were home?"

He didn't stop the audible groan from escaping. "I'm afraid we're not on the best of terms. We had a falling-out a couple of years ago. She never told you?"

"She just mentioned she never hears from you. You know her, she doesn't like talking behind people's backs. I don't think I've ever heard her speak unkindly about anyone."

"She got that from Mom." He pressed on his wound. "I'm afraid I inherited my father's temper."

"If you don't mind me asking, what was your fight about?" She shifted and her shoulder brushed against his. He couldn't stop the flush of feelings seeping through his body at her closeness.

He stood. Not only to distance himself from her but from the memory of the explosive argument he and Bree had had over Ivy. It was what severed their already shaky brother-sister tie.

"I'm sorry," Hazel said. "None of my business."

How could he tell her without revealing his fears? His deepest regrets? His father had always taught him to keep his emotions in check.

Never allow a woman to see you vulnerable.

He had done that once and it had almost cost him his life.

"It's not—"

"Boomer! Where are you?" Smokey's voice filtered into the cave.

Help had arrived.

Just in time to keep him from exposing something he wanted to stay hidden.

Hazel leaned on the railing at Hoyt Hideaway Ranch as she gingerly walked up the porch steps. Kane and the team he'd brought with him had helped them escape the wilderness with no further harm. Paramedic Evan Carson had once again cleaned up her cut and reprimanded her for not going to the hospital earlier. He had also confirmed a bullet had grazed Mitchell's left side, but he suggested they both get checked out at the hospital. Their journey down the mountain trail to the park station had been tricky, but they'd made it within an hour. However, their stay at the hospital had taken more time than Hazel's body could endure and she couldn't wait to climb into her bed.

If only her son could crawl into his. Guilt clawed at her for leaving him alone somewhere out in the forest and for causing Mitchell to get shot. She should have left when she'd first agreed to. He never would have gotten hurt. The shame threatened to send her over the edge, but she held on to a sliver of hope. Who was she kidding? She was barely grasping that thread.

"Are you sure your father won't mind that I stay in one of his cabins?" Mitchell's footfall thumped on the bottom step.

"Too bad if he does." Hazel's testy mood revealed sleep deprivation.

The front door burst open and Erica Hoyt flew onto the porch, bringing her daughter into an embrace. "Hazel! I'm so glad you're okay."

Hazel failed to hold her emotions in any longer and burst into tears. "Mama, I failed Jackson. He's still out there somewhere. What kind of mother abandons her child in need?" Her words came out in between sobs.

Her mother pushed her back and held her at arm's length. "The kind who takes time to put her safety mask on first. That's what they teach you on planes, remember? Secure yourself to help others. Love, you almost died for your son today. *That's* the kind of mother you are."

Hazel fell back into the arms of the woman she respected the most in this world. Her mother always knew what to say.

Frank Hoyt approached from around the ranch house,

shotgun in hand. "You still took unnecessary risks." He failed to curb his anger.

Hazel gazed at the man who continually belittled her at every opportunity.

"Frank, stop," her mother said. "That's no way to talk to your daughter, especially around a guest." She addressed Mitchell. "Good to see you again, son."

He nodded. "You too, Mrs. Hoyt. Just wish it was under better circumstances."

"It's Erica, and you're welcome here anytime."

"I appreciate it. My condo is two towns over and I'm afraid I wouldn't have made it in the state I'm in." He clutched his side. "Plus the doctor put me on strong meds and said I couldn't drive for a few hours."

She placed her hand on his arm. "I'm also sorry to hear of your dear mother's death. I know it's been a year, but I haven't seen you since."

"Thank you."

"Frank, help Mitchell inside. Your men have secured the perimeter, so I'm sure we're safe." Her mother wrapped her arm around Hazel's waist. "Let's get you settled with a little nourishment and then rest."

Hazel melted into her mother's touch. Her mama bear's hold encircled her like a security blanket and Hazel never wanted to leave. If her father wasn't like a prickly cactus, they just might get along better. Hazel's heart ached for his approval every day. She had tried to prove herself to him for years, but for some reason he remained distant from his children ever since Hazel's younger brother Kyle died. Well, all of them except her older sister, Jayla. They had mended their relationship after Jayla's near death from an avalanche, but even after coaxing Hazel to see her father's soft side, Jayla couldn't get her sister to concede. The pain of his brutal treatment of Hazel, his second oldest daughter, cut too deep. The scars remained etched in her mind.

Hazel ignored Frank Hoyt's mumblings behind her and let her mother lead her to the ranch's enormous living room where she had placed blankets over the comfy plaid couch and matching chair.

"Stay here, love. I'm gonna get you both a bite to eat." Her mother pointed to the chair across from Hazel. "Frank, help Mitchell sit."

Her father obeyed.

Hazel shifted to release the pressure on her wound. "But, Mom—"

"No *buts*, young lady. I realize it's the wee hours of the morning now, but you need something in your stomach before you head to bed. You've gone most of the day without food. You will do your son no good if we don't get some strength back into you. Tomorrow is a new day. Remember, His mercies are new every morning." Her mother caressed Hazel's cheek. "Be right back."

Warmth flowed through Hazel. Jayla had often said God gifted their mother with a direct line to His thoughts and words. Hazel agreed with her sister's assessment.

If only Hazel possessed the same line to God.

However, she had not only failed her son today but her Savior. Would He forgive her foolishness?

Her father walked over to the floor-to-ceiling bookcase and opened a drawer. "I know you both lost your cell phones, so I had my ranch hands get you new ones." He handed them both a device. "Stay out of the rivers."

"Thank you, sir." Mitchell stuffed his in his pocket.

"Hazel, as your mother said, I've stationed men around the property. I want you to be safe. No one will get by my ranch hands. Mitchell, we've prepared a cabin at the back

of the ranch for you. You'll be very comfortable there."
Her father sat on the other end of the long couch.

"Thanks again, sir," Mitchell said. "I appreciate your
generosity."

"No problem." He released the couch's lever and re-
clined. "Hazel, I can't believe you risked your life today
even after I warned you not to. When will you listen to
me? Mitchell got shot because of your stupidity."

Hazel sunk back into the plush couch. She was too
tired to argue because no one ever won an argument with
Frank Hoyt.

But…in this case, he was right. Mitchell could have
died today. Because of her. Guilt stabbed her along with
the piercing pain in her side. She should have returned to
the park station. Mitchell only remained in the forest because of her. He still thought of her as a little sister, wanting to protect her.

Why did that bother her so much?

You know why. Her crush on her best friend's older
brother had reawakened the moment she saw him coming
to rescue her from Firebug.

Was that even possible?

Mitchell leaned forward. "Sir, that's not true. I chose
to stay. Please don't be so hard on her."

Her father waggled a finger toward Mitchell. "Stay out
of this. You were both foolish." He turned to Hazel. "I realize you wanted to find my Bear Cub, but you need to
think with a clear mind."

Hazel held the armrest in a vise grip and counted to ten
slowly. Yes, her father was right about risking Mitchell's
life, but her mistakes were that—*her mistakes.* "Dad, I'm
no longer your little girl. I'm an adult and if I make mistakes, you need to stop chastising me for them. You can't
control everyone and everything. I'm tired of you bully-

ing me." She anchored herself on the armrest and pushed into a standing position. "Tell Mom to bring my food to my room. I can't take any more of your mood, Dad. I'm exhausted." She hated to be rude, but this man brought out the worst in her.

Hazel addressed Mitchell. "Night. Get some rest."

He smiled his lopsided grin and nodded.

Hazel suppressed the emotion rising from the man's captivating smile and turned to hide the redness flushing her face.

After eating a bowl of oatmeal her mother had brought to her room, Hazel settled under her toasty red-green-and-blue plaid comforter. She reached over and snatched the cell phone her father had given her. It was too late to call her best friend, but she wanted to at least text her. She entered Bree's number and keyed in a message.

B, this is my new #. Old phone in the river. Long story. U back from ur trip? Pls pray for J. He's missing. Worried sick. Why didn't u tell me Mitchell was back? Call me when u can. <3 u
H.

The thought of her son being alone in the wilderness brought a fresh bunch of tears and she buried her face into her pillow, sobbing. Fear for Jackson had finally overwhelmed her and she let the tears flow in private, calling out to God.

Father, please keep Jackson safe and warm tonight. I'm sorry I failed You.

Peace warmed her body, and she surrendered into God's embrace, letting His protection settle over her. It was as if He placed a kiss on her cheek, and rocked her to sleep.

* * *

A creak outside her door jolted Hazel awake, and she struggled to sit up. Her medication-induced foggy mind failed to assess the situation. She glanced at the clock. Had she really only been asleep for two hours? She stilled, waiting to see if she'd imagined the noise. It sounded again. The aged hardwood floor in front of her room always announced someone's presence.

Her family knew to sidestep the squeak. Something wasn't right.

Her door slowly opened, and a hand appeared. A knife glistened in the glow coming from a nightlight near the front of her room.

She stiffened.

How had the perp eluded her father's men?

She rolled and stumbled to the floor. Hazel attempted to stand, but her weakened legs wouldn't cooperate. She opened her mouth, but her scream lodged in her throat.

A masked figure stepped into the room and closed the door. "You can never escape me, Hazel. This time you die."

She didn't recognize the raspy, whispered voice.

Lord, give me strength.

She mustered courage and slowly stood. "Dad, help!" Finally, words came from her mouth, but would her delayed scream be in time for someone to save her?

"You think Frank Hoyt can rescue you now?"

"Who are you?"

"Someone you'd never guess."

Hazel struggled to identify the person. Somehow, they had disguised their voice. "Why me and why do you want my son?" She had to keep the person talking to give her father time to respond.

If he'd heard her at all.

"That's our little secret."

Our? What did that mean?

"Are you the Rocky Mountain Firebug?" she asked.

"Maybe. Maybe not." The person marched forward. "No more chitchat. Your time is up. Then I'll kill your boyfriend."

Hazel screamed. "No!"

Footfalls pounded down the hallway seconds before her door burst open. "Pumpkin!"

Her father had come to save her.

Frank Hoyt raised his shotgun. "Hold it there!"

The attacker bolted to the door that led to Hazel's patio, hit the lock and thrust it open, racing into the night.

"Go, Dad. Get him! He's also after Mitchell." Hazel's energy left her, and she dropped onto the bed.

"Are you okay?"

"Yes. Go!"

Her father dashed through the open patio door, his gun raised.

Hazel slipped onto the floor and kneeled in front of her bed, her hands folded into a prayer position. "Lord, protect our family. Save Mitchell."

Would her Heavenly Father hear her cry?

EIGHT

Mitchell sat upright in the cabin's bed. Was someone yelling his name or was he confusing it with the nightmare plaguing his dreams? He'd been searching in caves for Hazel and Jackson. When he finally found them, a bear had appeared and Hazel had shouted his name.

"Mitchell!"

Definitely not his dream. No, Frank Hoyt was calling him. Why?

The thundering sound of horses stampeding permeated the cabin. He swung his legs over the bed and flinched. Medication had only dulled the pain from his gunshot wound. He inhaled and took caution as he stood before shuffling to the window.

Frank ran toward his cabin, shotgun in hand.

Behind him, their stable was engulfed in flames.

Mitchell put on the fresh T-shirt Frank had given him, threw on cargo pants, and stepped into his work boots. He opened the door as the man arrived at the entrance. "What's going on?"

"Someone just tried to kill Hazel and was coming for you next." The man's words came in between ragged breaths. "They set the stable on fire."

"Where are your men?"

"Fighting the fire. We need your expertise. Do you have

strength to help?" Frank's widened eyes matched the pleading tone in his voice.

"I'll find it. Have you called 9-1-1?"

Frank nodded. "But you know how small this town is. They're tending to another fire."

Coincidence? Or had Firebug specifically diverted them from coming to the Hoyt Hideaway Ranch? Was that his plan all along? "Let me call my men in. They're wildland firefighters, but they know fires." Mitchell snatched his radio from the nightstand and turned to their unit's channel. "Team, Boomer here. Need assistance at Hoyt Hideaway Ranch. Bowhead Springs FD unavailable. Stables on fire. Bring equipment."

Silence stilled the room as they waited for a response.

The radio popped. "Princess here. Our ETA is fifteen minutes."

"Get here as fast as you can." Mitchell clipped the radio onto his belt. "Let's grab your hoses."

Frank nodded and raised his gun. "Stay behind me in case the suspect is still on the grounds."

He followed Frank out into the night.

Shouts greeted him, and in the distance, Mitchell noted Hazel huddled in her mother's arms, watching as their beloved stable blazed.

Would this family get a break today, Lord? Please stop this maniac. Whoever he is.

Not that God would listen to him, but he had to try.

Frank Hoyt stared at the flames as if mesmerized by the dancing embers.

Mitchell understood. Fires can captivate anyone and hold them hostage, but right now, Mitchell required the man's attention.

He snapped his fingers. "Frank, get your men to bring the hoses around. We'll fight it that way until my team arrives. Get me shovels too." He pointed to a group of horses who had barreled through the open fence. "You need to round the rest of your horses up. Looks like the suspect opened the gate, probably to create a distraction."

The man straightened before springing into action.

Mitchell approached Hazel and Erica. "You both okay?"

"Dad saved my life." Hazel's whispered words could barely be heard over the fire. "The attacker was going to stab me. Same as before. It had to be Firebug."

Mitchell's muscles tensed.

"Can you stop this blaze?" Erica asked.

"My team is inbound and Frank's getting your hoses. Apparently, Bowhead Springs firefighters are busy fighting another inferno." He pinched the bridge of his nose. "I'm guessing that's Firebug's doing. He wanted to keep emergency crews busy."

Hazel's jaw dropped. "He would've had to do that before coming here. Do you really think they're specifically targeting the Hoyt family?"

"No, I believe they're after you."

She latched on to his arm. "You too. Firebug told me he was going to kill you after he was finished with me. We're getting in his way."

"Thank God your father heard you scream." Erica wrapped her housecoat tighter around her body. "I just don't understand how he got by all of Frank's men."

"Are they trained in security?" Mitchell noted some of the ranch hands trying to corral the horses that hadn't escaped through the fence.

"A couple are ex-military. Frank found them knocked out cold and their radios missing." Erica scratched her head. "How did Firebug know to target them specifically?"

Mitchell drew in a hoarse breath. "Firebug somehow knows your ranch men or—" Dare he finish his thought?

Hazel's eyes widened. "Or one of them is working for Firebug."

"No way would my men betray me," Frank said as he approached, shovels in hand. "There has to be another explanation."

"We can figure it out later." Mitchell grabbed one of the shovels. "I'm going to dig a control line around the stables to prevent the fire from spreading. It's what we do in wildfires."

"I'll help." Frank pointed to the south side of the building. "Rusty is coming with the hose." He turned to Hazel. "Work with my ranch hand John to get the horses into the south paddock."

Two hours later, with the help of his Micmore unit, Mitchell had put out the fire and contained it from spreading to the trees or the Hoyt Hideaway Ranch's other buildings. The Bowhead Springs firefighters had finally arrived and ensured the fire was extinguished. Mitchell and his crew were proficient, and they worked well under pressure. Even Frank Hoyt's pressure to save his ranch.

Yes, the man could be rough on his daughter, but he showed his appreciation to Mitchell's unit by having his wife put out a huge breakfast spread. The woman was recognized in the area for her cooking and his team enjoyed every bite.

Mitchell sipped his coffee and leaned on the porch, enjoying the breathtaking view overlooking Micmore National Park. The sun kissed the mountain, creating a pink-purple glow as it rose over the peak. The only remnants of yesterday's storm were raindrops on the trees, glistening in the dawn's rays.

His mercies are new every morning.

Were the words Erica had spoken last night true? Did God's mercies renew every morning? Would God be merciful and help them find the boys today? Would He show His faithfulness?

These questions baffled Mitchell plus many more, especially when it came to good versus evil. How could a merciful God allow such hate in the world?

"You're deep in thought." Hazel rested against the railing, steam rising from her coffee.

Mitchell breathed in, loving her fresh lavender scent. Obviously, she'd cleaned herself up, as the captivating aroma had replaced the smoky smell. It was one he could get used to.

He, on the other hand, still reeked of fire. "I was just enjoying the sunrise."

She sipped her coffee. "This view never grows old. It's why I stayed here."

"I don't blame you. Plus the ranch has wide open spaces for Jack—"

He stopped. *Mitchell, how could you be so insensitive?*

She smiled. "You can say it. I agree. Jackson loves this place." A frown replaced her smile. "Just wish my dad wasn't so tough on both of us."

"He's hard on Jackson too?"

"Yup. 'Just teaching the boy how to make it in the outdoors. It will keep him safe.'" She changed her voice to match Frank's.

Mitchell suppressed a chuckle. She really sounded like her father.

Hazel stared toward the mountain peak, her smile fading. "I guess he was right. Everything he taught Jackson will help him right now. At least, I pray it does." She rolled her shoulders and pushed off the railing. "I want to get the search going again. Daybreak has arrived."

"Are you feeling up to it? How's your side?"

"Fine. Yours?"

"Sore, but I'll be okay. I want to help."

The door opened, and Frank walked onto the patio. "The search parties are gathering in thirty minutes."

"Good." Mitchell finished his coffee and turned to Hazel. "I'm going to get cleaned up and I'll meet—"

His radio squawked. "Boomer, report."

"My boss. I gotta take this." Mitchell raised the device and bounded down the steps. "I'm here. Fire is out and we're getting ready to start looking for the boys, boss."

"What about your unit duties? I just got a call about a wildfire east of you on Greenock Mountain."

Mitchell's side throbbed. "Sir, I'm not sure my injury will allow me to lug equipment and—"

"I'm not asking you to do heavy labor. Let your team do that. I'm asking you to set up a temporary EOC and command your group. I want you close to the fire, so you can report firsthand information. Get to Greenock Mountain now or I'll make good on my promise to replace you." He clicked off.

Mitchell turned and observed Hazel sipping her coffee. She almost had a serene look, even with her son still missing. How was that possible?

He sighed at his dilemma. If he didn't report for duty, he'd lose his job, but how could he desert her in her hour of need?

Plus a maniac was still out there trying to kill her.

Hazel shuddered as a flood of angst crawled down her spine. Standing in front of the warden station's pegboard, she studied the red pins on the map. Each one indicated a specific, searched location in Micmore National Park. The party had covered a lot of ground, but even with the help of SAR dogs, no one had spotted the boys. After Mitchell left to fight a wildfire on the other end of their massive park, she arrived at her station early to develop an attack plan, but first she had to see where the teams had been. Not that they could write those locations off, because the boys would more than likely move around. She leaned closer for a better look, fingering her son's favorite superhero ball cap hanging from her belt loop. Jackson had worn the hat the day before he'd left on his camping trip. She'd brought it along, hoping dogs would once again catch his scent.

"Where are you, Jackson?" *Lord, please show me where to start. Give me strength and be with Mitchell. Help him put out the wildfire.*

Her cell phone dinged, announcing a text. She took out the new device from her pocket and swiped. Mitchell. *Interesting timing, Lord.*

Another fire set by Firebug. Witness spotted someone planting a candle in the brush and called it in. Blaze is out of control and heading your way. Team working at containment. Stay safe.

Hazel squared her shoulders, determination seeping into her muscles and giving her strength. Today she would find Jackson and the boys before Firebug destroyed their national park.

Her cell phone buzzed. "Warden Hoyt here."

"Please tell me what's going on with Jackson." Bree's frantic voice boomed over the airwaves. "I just got back this morning."

Hazel put Bree on speakerphone. "So good to hear your voice. I've missed you." She plunked herself into a nearby chair. "I could use one of your hugs right now."

Bree's tall figure towered over Hazel's petite frame. When Bree hugged her, it was like nestling into a teddy bear's arms.

"Tell me what's going on, sweet lady."

"You haven't talked to Mitchell yet?" Hazel asked.

"I'm afraid we're not on speaking terms much lately, so no. That's why I didn't mention he was back. He arrived after I had left on my mission trip. Where's Jackson?"

Hazel longed to know why the brother and sister were on the outs, but right now, she had other things to ponder. "Missing with his scout team." Tears threatened to fall as she told her friend of yesterday's events and the hair-raising experience of getting stabbed, shot at and barricaded in a burning cabin. No wonder Hazel's body felt like a truck had run her down at full speed.

Bree whistled. "Oh, my. I'm coming over."

Hazel stood and walked back to the corkboard. "You just got back. Didn't you fly all night?"

"I did, but you're more important to me than sleep."

"No, B. You rest first. Come later. I'm not sure yet where we're searching anyway." As much as Hazel longed to see her friend, Bree required rest before she even attempted a search and rescue. Micmore National Park had too many cliffs and too much rugged terrain for anyone sleep-deprived.

Bree exhaled. "Fine. I'll text you once I get up. Then I'm coming."

"Sounds good. Talk to you later. Love you. Glad you're home."

"You too. I'd say have a Jesus-filled day, but now is probably not the time." She let out a moan. "But He is right here."

Hazel smiled at her friend's expression. Bree was known for the chipper line, but no, it wasn't what Hazel wanted to hear. *Why can't I give You control over Jackson, Lord?*

"Thanks, B. Talk to you later." She clicked off the call and picked up a marker. She circled different locations on the map.

"We've already searched those."

She startled at her father's voice, booming in the small room. Hazel had been in such deep thought, she'd missed his approach. "I realize that, Dad, but I know my son. If he's hiding from Firebug, those are the spots he'd go to." She circled a few more that hadn't been marked by a pin. "Plus these."

He pointed to an area close to Greenock Mountain. "I just got off the phone with Carey Morgan. We know that's where Mitchell's unit is working at containing the fire. If Firebug has kidnapped the boys, we may want to send a couple of parties there."

"Hawkweed Trail? That's too close to the fire. I don't feel the boys would have gone that far. I just don't understand why Jackson hasn't tried to get to the station. He knows the park. Is he lost?"

"Possibly. Micmore National Park is huge. You take the wrong turn and you can get disoriented." He hesitated. "Or Firebug has them."

"Dad, please don't say that. We don't know if he has them." Hazel massaged her tight neck muscles. "Have you heard anything from Stein's forensics team dispatched to the cabin to recover Stan's body?"

"Sergeant Stein told me the body was badly burned, but said his team mentioned you and Mitchell did a great job of containing the fire. He doubts his forensics unit will find any fingerprints. He'll keep me updated on any developments as he's in constant contact with them."

A question emerged in Hazel's mind. "Why was Stan at the cabin by himself?"

"No idea. Shari sent him and a team to that area after you gave us your last location, before your canoe tipped." Her father filled his canteen from the water cooler. "The other two in the party said he disappeared after he claimed to have seen the vagrant. They couldn't find him and figured he'd make his way back alone."

"We must find that vagrant, Dad. He may know something."

"Agreed, but the man keeps evading us. Somehow. I'm beginning to wonder if he actually exists, since none of our park workers have spoken with him."

Hazel rubbed her temple, warding off a migraine threatening to emerge. "Well, many campers have spotted him, so he's definitely out there. I don't think they would have made him up."

"Catch him. I want him out of my park!"

"Dad, I'm trying to find my son. Why—"

The front screen door slammed and Nora walked into the room. "Morning."

Hazel was thankful for her friend's interruption. Her dad's abrupt attitude grated on Hazel's nerves. She had more things to think about than someone taking refuge in their park.

Her father tipped his hat in greeting, then turned to Hazel. "I'm going to talk to the others now outside. Don't be late. We need to get the search going again."

Yes, Dad.

Hazel set her thoughts aside and gathered Nora into a bear hug. "Are you okay? Firebug hit you hard yesterday."

"I'm fine and I want to help with the search." Nora pushed back from Hazel and walked to the pegboard. "I feel so guilty that Firebug got the drop on me. I need to make it right."

"Nora, it's not your fault. This person is pure evil. How someone can destroy wildlife and kill people is beyond me." *And God, why do You allow it?*

Nora turned from gazing at the map. "Why do you think he's doing it?"

"That's an excellent question, my friend. I also don't know why he's targeting me and my son." Hazel circled one more place on the map and slid the marker back into its slot. She took a picture of the pegboard.

"Well, I hope we catch him soon and find the boys."

"Me too." Hazel stocked her duty belt with a flashlight, ammo, jackknife, bear spray and bug repellent. "Okay, if you're coming, I want you to stay close to me. No hero stuff today, okay?"

Nora saluted. "Yes, Warden Hoyt."

Hazel placed her hands on her hips. "Did I just sound like my father?"

"Yup." Nora's face contorted for a split second before she snickered.

But what was the odd expression that flashed on her face?

Anger toward Frank Hoyt?

Hazel sloughed off Nora's reaction and put on her hat. After all, didn't most people have the same opinion of her father? Her coworkers often complained to Hazel about his stern attitude. She held the door open for her friend. "Let's go."

Hazel followed Nora down the steps and approached the group of people gathered around her father. A team of SAR workers had their dogs on alert. The animals barked as if communicating to the group they were ready for action.

Lord, help the dogs catch the boys' scent. But was that possible after yesterday's fierce storm? She gulped in a breath and unhooked Jackson's hat, turning to Nora. "I'm going to give this to the handler."

Hazel scrambled over to the team's position and approached the man holding the leash of a bloodhound. She held out Jackson's cap. "Can you use this to catch my son's scent?"

"Yes, ma'am. Duke here is the best of the best. I'm Max." The young man's wiry red curls stuck out from his cap's rim. "We're just waiting for final instructions from Supervisor Hoyt."

"Thank you." Hazel turned back to put her attention on her father as he addressed the search party.

"Sergeant Stein, the leader of our local police station, has sent constables to help in our search," her father said. "I've called in all of our wardens. They are armed and we're placing one in each of your groups. We are not taking any risks today, folks. These people are dangerous." He gestured toward the picnic table equipped with water bottles and snacks. "It's gonna be another warm day, so be sure to grab supplies. This odd heat wave is tormenting our region and we don't want anyone fainting." He clapped. "Okay, head out. Stay alert. Stay alive. Find those boys."

He approached Hazel. "I'm coming with you and Nora. We're going to Hawkweed Trail. We'll take the UTVs. It'll be quicker."

"But, Dad, Jackson wouldn't go there. It's too far." Why wouldn't her father listen to her?

He waggled his finger in her face. "Don't argue. We need to be sure they're not there."

Hazel gnawed on her lip, biting back the retort she wanted to say. However, it wouldn't do any good to debate her father's thinking. She just prayed they'd be safe from the raging fire. "I gave the handler Jackson's favorite hat."

Her father motioned to Max. "Let's see what Duke here does."

The man bent down and held the ball cap under the bloodhound's nose. "Duke, search!"

The dog woofed and bolted in a northerly direction.

Straight toward Hawkweed Trail, where her father said they should go.

Hope flowed through her veins and she sent Mitchell a quick text, telling him they were headed his way.

Moments later, Hazel guided her UTV onto Hawkweed Trail with Nora in the passenger seat.

Her father rode ahead of them, glancing over his shoulder. "Come on, we have lots of ground to cover in a short time frame," he yelled into the radio.

Hazel gritted her teeth and accelerated.

After thirty minutes of riding toward Hawkweed Trail, Hazel brought her UTV to a stop beside her father.

He clicked off his cell phone, a forlorn expression resting on his handsome face.

"What's going on, Dad?" Her heartbeat increased, sending agony throughout her body. "Please tell me Jackson is okay."

"Got a report Duke turned in a different direction, following a scent. The team will keep me updated. That phone call was Stein. The fire chief found the cause of the cabin's fire. Someone had tossed a gas can in the woods. Forensics lifted a print belonging to a known felon. Tommy Alcorn."

Hazel gulped in an audible breath. "Isn't he the one who kidnapped a little girl last year? He's out of jail already?"

"Escaped yesterday morning. Police have put a BOLO out but haven't found him yet." Her father's cell phone chimed, and he checked the screen. "Stein sent me a picture. Sending it to you now."

Hazel's phone buzzed, and she removed it from her vest's front pocket, studying the man's face before passing the device to Nora.

Her friend glimpsed at the photo. "Wait a minute. I need a better look." Nora clicked on the picture and enlarged it, peering closer.

"What do you see?" Hazel asked.

Nora's jaw dropped. "I saw him this morning in the

crowd at the warden station. His hair is different, but it's him. His hat partially hid his face, but I recognize his quirky smile because he flirted with me."

Hazel's breakfast turned hard as a rock, rotting her stomach. "What? He's out there searching for my boy? How was he allowed on the team?"

Nora handed Hazel back her phone. "Now that I think about it, he lingered off to the side. Not sure he was actually on a team."

Hazel's dad once again examined the picture. "She's right. I remember him now. Friendly chap. Asked many questions about the search." He hit a button. "I'm calling Stein back. I can't believe he was right under my nose and I didn't know it."

Hope and dread merged inside Hazel, creating a flurry of emotions. Dread because of the fact this man lurked among their teams, but hope they may be close to catching the Rocky Mountain Firebug. "Wait. Do you think he could be Firebug?"

"Anything's possible." Her father rode away as he spoke on his cell phone.

Hazel sent the picture to Mitchell along with a text.

Keep an eye out for this person possibly posing as one of our searchers. Could be Firebug.

Seconds later, a response dinged her phone.

I just saw this man talking to Smokey, north of the fork in Hawkweed Trail.

She grimaced and keyed in another message.

Heading your way. Need to speak with Kane.

Hazel's adrenaline spiked, and she pressed her radio button. "Dad! Mitchell said they just saw Tommy. Come on!" She sped down the trail.

Were they moments away from finding the boys and stopping the serial arsonist plaguing their region?

NINE

Mitchell's pulse magnified as Hazel's message revealed more danger in his already treacherous situation. He stuffed his cell phone back into his pocket and tried hard to ignore his throbbing side. The wildfire had not only zapped his energy but had increased his pain level. However, he would not resort to taking more pills. They made him too groggy, and he required alert senses. Mitchell studied the smoke in the distance from his command center. Thankfully, his team had slowed the fire's spread, but if the wind shifted again, they could be in trouble. He withdrew his radio and pressed the button. "Smokey, report your location."

Mitchell had to find and subdue Tommy Alcorn until the police arrived. The man obviously had an interest in finding Jackson and the boys. Was he Firebug?

"A few kilometers south of your position. Why?" Smokey's rough voice relayed his irritation.

Mitchell ignored his coworker's attitude. "The man you spoke with a few minutes ago. Where is he?"

"Tom-Tom? He just left to search for the boys after flirting big-time with Princess. Why do you ask?"

A shiver entwined its way down Mitchell's spine as suspicions crept into his mind. Why hadn't Smokey reported the fugitive if he knew who he was?

"He escaped from prison, and you didn't stop him?"

Grumbles riddled the airwaves. "He told me he served his time and got out on parole. He wanted to help find Jackson."

Mitchell's neck muscles throbbed. "He only named Jackson?"

"Yes, he wanted to help get him back to his mother."

Strange, since there were other boys missing. Something wasn't right. Once again, Mitchell pressed his radio button. "When did you last see Tommy?"

"Five minutes ago."

"Okay. Stay alert. He's dangerous. I need you at the EOC. Stat."

A commotion sounded through the radio, followed by a lengthy break in the conversation.

Mitchell bristled. "Smokey? Did you get that?"

"Sorry, was moving farther down the control line. Boomer, we need to put this fire out and not waste time talking. Why do you need me there?"

The sound of inbound UTVs caught Mitchell's attention, and he turned. Two vehicles appeared over the knoll. "Hazel needs to ask you some questions. Please, just do it." He tensed as he waited for more resistance.

"Fine. Be there shortly."

Mitchell clenched his jaw, and after contacting Princess to take over for Smokey, he stuffed his radio back onto his belt. Seeing Hazel this close to a fire prickled at Mitchell. Why had her father insisted on bringing her here? It made little sense.

Then again, nothing made sense when it came to Frank Hoyt. Mitchell approached the group. "Why are you all this close to a fire? You must leave the area now. It's too dangerous."

The group climbed off their UTVs.

Frank strode forward. "I'm not leaving until we've checked your area for the boys. Plus we want to talk to Smokey."

Hazel yanked on her father's arm. "Dad, you're not helping matters." She mouthed "sorry" to Mitchell.

He marveled at how beautiful she looked even in a warden's uniform. Her cute cowboy-like hat only added to his sudden attraction toward his little sister's best friend. Why had she been in his head ever since she came back into his life yesterday? *You know why.* She had not only grown into a beautiful woman but her kind demeanor enticed him further. *Focus. You have a job to do and it's not fantasizing about a woman.* Plus she probably only viewed him as an older brother. He cleared his throat, putting his attention back to where it should be. "Have there been any sightings of them?"

"We have many search parties scouring the park." Hazel gestured toward the distant smoke. "Where's the fire?"

Mitchell followed her gaze. "Too close. My crew's doing a good job of containing it, but things can change in an instant with wildfires."

Nora stepped forward. "Guys, we need to turn back. We're putting ourselves at risk."

"She's right," Mitchell said. "I haven't seen any signs of the boys and I've been here since six."

Smokey arrived on the utility vehicle and dismounted. "Boomer, I'm here. What do you want? I don't have much time. This fire won't go out on its own."

Frank Hoyt folded his arms across his chest. "You know Tommy Alcorn?"

"Went to high school together."

"Police are on their way here and want to talk to you." Frank waggled his finger in Smokey's face. "You let an escaped criminal go free."

Smokey's eyes widened, and he stumbled backward. "I didn't know that before Mitchell told me. Tom-Tom was in prison a few towns over and I haven't heard from him in ages. He told me he got paroled." The firefighter's gaze shifted to the ground, evading any further eye contact.

Suspicion prickled the hairs at the back of Mitchell's neck. Smokey wasn't being totally truthful. What was he hiding?

"Did he say why he joined the search for the boys?" Hazel asked. "Seems kind of odd when he was convicted of kidnapping a little girl about Jackson's age."

Smokey kept his gaze at his feet. "He said he wanted to get Jackson back to his mother. Then we shot the breeze for a few minutes before he rejoined his party."

A gust caught Hazel's hat, and she pushed it farther down on her head. "How long ago was this, and where did he go?"

"Ten minutes. He took Hawkweed Trail."

Mitchell marched into Smokey's personal space. "What aren't you telling us?"

The man's head whipped up, and his eyes narrowed. "Nothing, Boomer. That's all I know."

Mitchell analyzed his coworker's face. His explanation felt off. In what way, Mitchell couldn't tell.

Hazel addressed Smokey. "He's a kidnapper, but do you think he would set these fires?"

His eyes bulged. "You think Tom-Tom is Firebug? No way."

"Why do you say that?" Mitchell asked. "How well do you know him?"

"Well, he always was different. Came from a rough home life, but I don't think he'd set fires like this."

Nora huffed. "No excuse for kidnapping. My father left us for another woman when I was young. Then my mother killed herself. You don't see me in prison."

A wave of smoke assaulted the area.

Mitchell's muscles once again knotted. "Guys, you need to get out of here."

Frank's radio squawked.

"Hoyt, it's Stein. Officers are ten minutes from your south entrance."

Frank pressed the button. "Copy that. On my way with a witness." He pointed to Smokey. "You're coming with me. The police will want to know everything you and Tommy spoke about."

Smokey scowled. "Fine, I'll meet you there." He hopped onto the UTV.

"Dad, I want to stay with Mitchell and search the area for the boys." Hazel turned to Nora. "You head back to the station and monitor our progress from there."

Nora bit her lip. "You can't stay either."

As much as Mitchell wanted Hazel's company, he agreed with Nora. "She's right. It's too dangerous. You need to let us extinguish the fire first."

Hazel placed her fisted hands on her hips, tilting her head. "You can't tell me what to do. I need to find my son, and if there's a remote possibility he's in the area, I need to check."

How could he reason with her? "That goes against all protocol, Hazel. I can't put you in danger."

"I already am. Danger of losing my only son."

He hissed through his teeth. "You are still just as stubborn as you were as a teenager."

"You can't argue with Mama Bear." Nora smirked.

"Plus she has a little of me in her." Frank mounted his UTV. "I'll report back what I find out." He rode off in the same direction as Smokey.

Mitch turned back to Hazel in time to see her glare at him and say, "I'm not leaving, Mitch."

He threw his arms in the air. "Fine, but you need to do exactly what I say when I say it." He inched closer to the petite brunette. "Understood?" Wait—had she just called him by his nickname? He liked the way it rolled off her tongue. *Focus, Mitch.*

"Of course."

Nora shook her head before riding back down the trail.

Mitchell's cell phone buzzed, and he collected it from his side pants pocket. He swiped the screen.

Get out of my wilderness or pay a hefty price. Will it be sweet Bree or the cute warden in the cowboy hat? Go home. Remember, I'm watching and if you don't leave now, someone dies.

Firebug.

Mitchell sucked in a breath and observed the area around his command center.

Where was the Rocky Mountain Firebug hiding?

Goosebumps needled across Hazel's arms like slivers of broken glass prickling her skin. She read the terror-stricken expression plaguing Mitchell's face. Something had happened. "What is it?" She braced herself for more bad news. *Please God, let it not be about Jackson.*

Mitchell raised his cell phone. "Text from Firebug."

"What? How did he get your number?" She leaned closer and read the message. "Where is he? We need to capture him. Now!"

Movement rustled the leaves in the tree line near Mitchell's command center. Seconds later, flames ignited in a bush. Hazel's adrenaline spiked, and she pointed. "Mitchell!"

Somehow, Firebug had snuck up on them and started

another fire in the bushes. Still holding her gun, Hazel gripped it tighter as she scanned the area, but nothing out of the ordinary appeared in her line of sight.

Mitchell grabbed a portable backpack pump. "Stay away. I need to stop the fire from moving toward the forest." He rushed toward the bush and sprayed the flames. As quickly as it had appeared, he extinguished the blaze.

Thank You, Lord.

Something glittered in the sunlight on the ground next to Mitchell. She holstered her weapon and approached. "What's beside you?" She pointed.

He scooped up the object and handed it to her. "A watch. Do you think it's Firebug's?"

Hazel's hand flew to her mouth, silencing a scream. She shook her head. "No, it's Jackson's. I gave it to him on his eighth birthday." She fell to the ground and sobbed. "That madman has my son."

Mitchell squatted beside her. "You don't know that for sure. From what I've seen so far, Firebug is a master manipulator. He may have planted it here to throw us off the scent."

She hopped upright. "Wait. Jackson may have left the watch as another bread crumb. Perhaps he is around here somewhere. I need to search."

Mitchell unhooked his radio. "I'm calling Princess. I need her to take the lead because I'm coming too."

"But what will your boss say? You're already on shaky ground."

"Don't care. Jackson's life is at stake, and I'm not leaving you alone out there with Tommy Alcorn on the loose."

Twenty minutes after Mitchell brought Princess up to speed at the command center, Hazel and Mitchell stopped at a campsite.

"Hello? Anyone here?" Hazel plunked down on the picnic table bench, removed her canteen and sipped before returning it to her backpack.

Mitchell approached the tent and opened the flap, peeking inside. "No one in there."

"Perhaps they went fishing." Hazel stood.

"Doubtful with the wildfire near here. We warned the campers, and most cleared out."

Movement from the forest drew Hazel's gaze. A figure darted between trees. She unholstered her gun. Not something she normally did in her own park, but today her son and the other boys were still out there. Alone with a maniac lurking.

"Mitchell, over there!" She raised her weapon and sped to the tree line.

"Wait!" he yelled.

Mitchell's footfalls pounded behind her, indicating he'd followed.

The suspect dashed from one tree to the next in a zigzag pattern. Hazel gripped her 9mm tighter, holding it in a downward, ready-mode position, like she'd been trained.

"Stop! We just want to talk." Hazel's words came out jumbled as she ran. She looked over her shoulder to catch a glimpse of Mitchell and spotted him through the trees. She turned back and concentrated on following the man. A pain jabbed her wound, but she ignored it and moved faster. She wouldn't let the injury Firebug inflicted on her slow her down. No, she'd catch this person and find her son.

Ahead, she noted the man leaning against a tree, doubled over, panting.

Was he hurt, or was this a ruse to capture Hazel?

She beelined toward a tree only yards away from the man, then slowed her pace and raised her gun. "Hold it there."

The man kept his head down, one arm wrapped around

his stomach, and the other hiding behind his back. "Help. I'm hurt."

"Show me your right hand." Hazel kept a tight grip on her weapon in a readied position. "Slowly."

"You can't stop him." He whipped out his right hand and raised a gun as he showed his face.

Tommy Alcorn.

The man sneered. "I'm not going back to prison. Sorry you have to die." His finger twitched on the trigger.

Hazel didn't hesitate, and fired, hitting him in his right shoulder.

He screamed and dropped his gun.

Hazel raced to his side and kicked the firearm out of his reach. "You're under arrest."

"You're only a park warden. You can't arrest me." He held on to his shoulder, blood seeping through his fingers.

"Don't be so sure," she said through her gritted teeth. Movement sounded behind her. She pivoted, keeping her weapon trained.

Mitchell raised his hands. "Just me."

"Don't do that." She motioned toward Tommy. "Help me get him to the campsite's picnic table over there."

"Aren't you calling in a paramedic for me?" Tommy asked.

Mitchell hurried to Hazel's side and hauled the man upright. "We will, but first we have some questions."

"Like what? I know nothing."

"Did you lock us in that cabin and set it on fire?" Mitchell asked.

"He told me to get rid of you," Tommy scoffed. "I almost succeeded."

Hazel holstered her gun and scooped up Tommy's weapon, stuffing it into the back of her uniform pants. She then helped guide the suspect to the picnic table. "Should we call you Firebug?"

The man's eyes widened. "What? No!"

Mitchell tilted his head. "You're not the Rocky Mountain Firebug?"

"How could I be, when I just escaped prison yesterday morning?"

Mitchell's shoulders slumped. "He's right, Hazel. Firebug started setting fires four weeks ago."

Hazel shifted her stance. "Then, tell me why you're out here so close to a wildfire."

"I'm helping in the search for Jackson. I pitched a tent near here."

"Why would a fugitive risk exposing his identity to look for the boys?" Hazel asked.

Mitchell addressed Tommy. "She's right. You're not telling us the truth. Who are you protecting?"

"Hazel, you there?" Her father's voice emanated from her radio.

Hazel pressed the button. "Go ahead, Dad."

"Stein interrogated Smokey. It took some coaxing, but he shared something he failed to mention earlier."

Mitchell jumped off the bench. "I knew he held information back. What is it?"

"Apparently, Tommy bragged to him he was coming into some money, but first he had to find a little boy. Smokey said Tommy threatened him if he said anything."

"That's a lie!" Tommy yelled.

"Wait. You have him there, Hazel?" her father asked.

Hazel walked away from Tommy and brought the radio to her mouth. "Yes, Dad. I wounded him. Send emergency services to our location. Two kilometers northeast of Mitchell's command center."

"Are you okay?"

"Fine. We're questioning him now."

"Hazel, don't do anything stupid!"

She fumed. Why did her father think she wasn't capable of protecting her park? "Dad, I have this under control. Please, just do as I ask."

"Be careful."

"Of course." She clicked off, walking back to their prisoner. "Tell me all about this cash you're getting. Did Firebug contract you to kidnap my son?"

"I'm telling you the truth. I don't know anything about that." He clutched his shoulder tighter. "Help me, please."

Mitchell leaned over Tommy and reached a hand out toward his shoulder. "Well, it's gonna hurt a lot more in seconds if you don't start giving us the right story."

Silence.

Mitchell's hand shifted closer.

"Okay! Okay! Don't touch me." Tommy stared at Hazel. "My cellmate told me about a huge score right up my alley. Said he found a way for me to get out of prison and score us both lots of cash. If I agreed, he'd set it up but take a cut. The plan was that Firebug would pose as a prison transport guard." He winced and breathed in.

"What happened?" Hazel asked.

"The plan executed perfectly. He bribed another guard, and once we got in the vehicle, he gave me a wad of cash and a picture of a boy I had to bring to him. Then I'd get the rest of the money."

Mitchell paced around the picnic table. "Why you? Why go through all that trouble to break you out when he could have gotten someone else or even himself to kidnap a boy? It doesn't make sense."

"He said his previous plan failed, and he had to try something different." Tommy snickered. "I guess I have a reputation for getting close to kids."

Heat bull-rushed Hazel at the thought of this man abducting Jackson and the other boys. "Show me the picture he gave you."

Tommy fished it from his pocket and handed it to her. Jackson's school picture.

She stumbled backward as thunder boomed in her temples. "No!"

"I take it that's your son? You're the woman they wanted to punish?"

Hazel pushed down the bile rising in her throat and drew her weapon, pointing it at Tommy. "Where is my son?"

"No idea! I couldn't find him."

"What's Fircbug's real name?" Mitchell asked.

"Don't know, but I can help you identify him. I know what he looks like."

Mitchell nudged him off the picnic bench. "Good. Let's walk."

The sound of rustling bushes behind Hazel nabbed her attention and she pivoted, raising her weapon.

But she was too late.

A flaming arrow whizzed through the air and struck Tommy's heart in a perfect bullseye.

The man dropped.

The Rocky Mountain Firebug had hit his target, silencing their only witness to his identity.

TEN

Mitchell tackled Hazel like a linebacker, knocking her to the ground to eliminate her as a mark from more arrows. His side screamed at him for executing such a bold move, but he wouldn't allow harm to come to Hazel. Not on his watch. Mitchell held his breath, waiting for more arrows, but none came.

"Mitch, I can't breathe. Move." Hazel pushed on his shoulders.

He rolled off her but kept low as he examined the forest. "Do you see any movement?"

"None." Hazel scrambled over to Tommy's body and patted down any remaining flames before checking his vitals. "He's gone. Any hopes of identifying Firebug died with him." She hung her head and rubbed her temples.

Mitchell read her body language, and her slumped shoulders revealed her feelings of defeat. Would she now lose hope in God's ability to help?

Like he had when Ivy did the unthinkable and tried to kill him? Mitchell had reached out to God, but only silence had returned when he cried out for help. The day Ivy buried him alive was the day Mitchell stopped trusting God.

Shouts followed by thudding footsteps announced the arrival of emergency services. Evan, the paramedic, along with his female partner and Constable Porter, bounded through the woods toward them.

Mitchell pushed himself upright.

Evan scurried over to them. "You guys okay?"

"Fine." Mitchell hissed a breath through his teeth. "However, dodging flaming arrows is dangerous." He gestured toward Tommy. "I'm afraid he didn't make it."

The female paramedic squatted in front of the body and placed her fingers on the man's neck. "He's right. No pulse."

Constable Porter circled the fallen man before kneeling. "What happened here? It appears he has both an arrow wound and a GSW to the shoulder."

"I'm afraid the GSW is from me," Hazel said. "He was about to shoot, but I fired first, wounding him. We secured his weapon and were questioning him when the flaming arrow came out of nowhere."

"A flaming arrow?" Constable Porter whistled. "Well, that's not something you see every day."

Hazel pointed. "It came from that direction. I suggest you get a team to examine the area."

The constable pressed the button on his shoulder radio. "Dispatch, send a team to my location." He walked away as he spoke further instructions into his radio.

Evan kneeled in front of Mitchell. "Can you show me your wound? I want to check it."

Mitchell lifted his shirt. "I'm sure it's fine. I just banged it when I fell."

"I'll be the judge of that." Evan pointed to his partner. "By the way, this is Vanessa. She's new to our team."

Mitchell nodded. "Nice to meet you."

"Likewise." She turned to Hazel. "I heard about the boys. I'm so sorry."

"Thank you." Hazel unhooked her radio. "Mitchell, I'm

going to contact Dad for an update on the search. Be right back."

Mitchell nodded. "Evan, did you guys run across anyone suspicious on your way here?"

"Nothing. Hazel must be worried sick." Evan peeled off Mitchell's bandage and palpated the area around the gunshot wound.

Mitchell inhaled sharply.

"Sorry, it appears fine. We'll put on a fresh bandage." Evan turned to Vanessa. "Call the ME. I've got this."

She nodded and stepped away from the group.

"How's your pain level?" Evan took out a bandage from his bag, and within a couple minutes, he'd replaced the soiled one.

Mitchell tucked his shirt into his waistband. "About a six, but I'll be fine."

"You should be resting. You don't want to get an infection."

"No time for that, with Firebug still out there and those boys missing. Not to mention keeping the wildfires under control." Mitchell's cell phone buzzed, and he fished it out of his pocket, then swiped the screen. Bree. Great. He wasn't sure he wanted to deal with her right now. The last time they spoke hadn't gone the greatest. He raised his phone. "Sorry, gotta take this. Thanks for your help."

"No prob. I'll go check on Vanessa's progress. If you see an infection in your wound, get medical attention. Stay safe." Evan walked over to where his partner stood, chatting on her phone.

Mitchell hit the talk button. "Hey, sis. You're back."

"Mitch, what's going on with Jackson? I want to help with the search." His sister's words came out groggy.

"Your flight just get in? You sound tired."

"A few hours ago. I caught some sleep, but now I want to help. Where are you guys? I can't get a hold of Hazel."

Mitchell pinched his brow. "Sis, it's not safe out here. There's an approaching wildfire and a killer on the loose."

"And boys missing. You left out that part. Hazel needs me and I won't let her down." Bree's frustrated tone filtered through the phone.

Mitchell didn't miss her emphasis on the word *her*, implying *he* had let Bree down. Why did his sister always bring the worst out in him? Their relationship had been shaky for years, but after Ivy tried to kill him, Bree had started smothering him, and then everything escalated after their precious mother's death. Mitchell had refused to do a eulogy after Bree kept hounding him, but he just couldn't bring himself to get up in front of people and display his emotions in public. His sorrow over his mother's death had run too deep, and he'd known he'd break down. Their mother-son bond had been severed, and Mitchell struggled with her loss every day.

Guilt over his disconnected relationship with Bree bothered him and he longed for her companionship again, but she had pushed God on him too much lately. He wasn't ready to come back to the God who had allowed both Ivy into his life and taken the one person on the planet who understood him the most—Tracy Booth. *Why did you take my mother so early?*

"Mitch, you still there?" Bree asked.

Hazel bounded toward him, and from her rigid body language, he surmised she carried bad news.

Her presence also reminded him of the sisterly connection Hazel and Bree had, and he wasn't about to get in between it. "Sorry, sis. We're near the Greenock Mountain Campsite. Please be careful. I gotta run."

"See you soon." She clicked off.

Mitchell stood. "What is it? What's wrong?"

She waved a map in the air. "Dad just told me Duke picked up a scent."

So, why the forlorn look? "That's good news, isn't it?"

She pointed to the map. "Not when it's on Fireweed Cliff Trail and—"

"Close to the wildfires." He pulled out his radio. "Let me contact my team for an update and we'll head there. You contact Bree. She just called and I told her to come here. Tell her to meet us at Greenock Junction."

First, he required his leader's approval, but he would not let Hazel down like he had his sister.

God, if You're really out there, find those boys and stop this madman.

Hazel twisted the cord bracelet Jackson had made for her, and her chest tightened as she thought of him being close to the cliffs of Greenock Mountain and near the blazing wildfire. That section of Micmore National Park was dangerous, and she'd told him never to go there for any reason. So what had driven her son to take that path? Or had Firebug caught up to them and pushed them in that direction? Hazel and Mitchell were now at the junction, waiting for Bree. She checked her watch. *Come on, Bree. We have to move.* Her friend had promised she'd be there, stat, but Hazel couldn't wait much longer.

Mitchell had talked his boss into letting him join the search since he could use his eyes in that region to monitor the growing wildfires as long as he kept him updated. His team was digging more control lines to stop the fire in its tracks.

She leaned against a tree and analyzed his handsome face as she listened for any search updates over her radio. Mitchell's short brown hair enhanced his clean-cut image, but it was his perfect lips that drew her eyes. What would it be like to kiss him? To linger in his powerful embrace?

Had she really just thought about that now? She had dreamed about kissing him when she was a teenager, but he had made it clear back then by his actions he only thought of her as a little sister. *Focus, Hazel. Nothing has changed. He will only ever think of you as a little sister.*

"Hazel!" Bree sped down the path toward them.

Hazel met her halfway and flung her arms around her best friend. "I'm so happy to see you." Her voice hitched and Hazel couldn't contain the tears.

"I'm so sorry about Jackson," Bree said.

Bree's teddy bear hug tightened, and Hazel rested in her friend's arms. "Sorry for being so emotional."

Bree rubbed Hazel's back. "It's me, sweet friend. Never apologize for that. We've been through so much together. Many times it's been the reverse and you've comforted me."

Hazel pushed away from the embrace and eyed Mitchell. He had reattached his radio and stood staring at them. His contorted expression spoke volumes. It wasn't a look of judgment. Longing? Hazel knew their brother-sister relationship was strained, but Bree hadn't given her all the details.

Okay, Hazel. Time to get it together and find your son. She cleared her throat. "Let's head to Fireweed Cliff Trail."

Mitchell approached. "Do I get a hug, sis?" He held out his arms.

Bree walked into his embrace. "Mitch, how are you?"

"Okay."

Hazel harrumphed. "Liar. He was shot yesterday."

Bree drew back. "You what?"

"Just a graze. I'm fine." He caressed her face. "It's good to see you."

"Hazel, what's your location?" Her father's voice blasted through the radio.

Hazel pressed the button. "At Greenock Junction. On our way now. Did Duke find anything?"

"We're still following him. Get here soon. Jackson will want his mother when we find him."

Lord, make it so. "On our way." She turned to her friend. "Bree, are you sure you're okay? You look exhausted."

Bree squeezed Hazel's shoulder. "I'm fine and I want to help search. I love your boy too, you know."

Her friend was like a second mother to Jackson. They had a strong bond. "I know. Mitchell, time to go?"

"Yes. Seems the police released Smokey and Morgan assigned him as the lead in putting out the fires." Mitchell gathered his equipment. "You can use a firefighter. Just in case."

"Let's go." Hazel adjusted her warden belt and attached her backpack, heading down the trail with one thing on her mind.

Find Jackson and the boys fast.

Twenty minutes later, Hazel's team reached the trailhead to Fireweed Cliff Trail. Her father, Nora and a small search party waited off to the side, studying a map.

"Dad, any updates?" Hazel held her breath, hoping for good news.

Her father held out the map and pointed. "These are the areas we've covered off."

"Where did Duke pick up Jackson's scent?" she asked.

"The last we've heard was right here." Her father had circled the spot in red. "Teams have searched the area, but so far, no sign of the boys."

Hazel's shoulders slumped, defeat locking her already tight muscles. They needed a break. She didn't want her son alone in the wilderness for another night. *God, please help.*

A hint of smoke swept in their direction and increased the trepidation coursing throughout Hazel's body. Quivers attacked her petite frame.

The wind had changed directions. Not good.

She pivoted and addressed Mitchell. "We need a fire update."

"Already on it." He pressed his radio button. "Princess, the wind has changed directions. Report."

"Control line is holding. For now," Princess said. "The weather is unpredictable today."

"Agreed. Keep me apprised. We're at Fireweed Cliff Trail. Get Smokey to request air tankers drop retardant. We need this fire out. Now. Before it gets worse and travels to our location." Mitchell's normal gentle tone hardened, then he sighed and raked his fingers through his hair. "Sorry, just a bit tense here."

Hazel understood the change in the normally kind man's demeanor. Emotions were at the breaking point. When would they snap?

"No prob, Boomer," Princess said. "I'll get aerial here. Smokey hasn't shown up yet."

Mitchell checked his watch and frowned. "They released him forty-five minutes ago. He should be there by now."

As if sensing the alarm in her brother, Bree moved to his side and squeezed his shoulder.

"I'll get Morgan on it. Stay safe. Princess out."

Mitchell tucked his radio back into its holder.

"He's probably just stuck in traffic," Bree said. "You know how that highway can get."

"She's right. The police station is downtown." Hazel doubted her own words. Bowhead Springs was only ten kilometers away from Micmore. A question formed. Had something happened to Kane Everson or was he somehow involved and went into hiding?

Mitchell placed his hands on his hips. "You both realize—"

Excessive barking sounded nearby, interrupting the conversation.

"Supervisor Hoyt, this is Max. Duke has found something." The K-9 handler paused. "He's digging."

Hazel's father pivoted, and his horror-struck gaze met hers.

She gasped.

Had Duke found her son?

No, Lord!

Hazel sprinted toward the direction of the dog's low bark that changed to a howl.

ELEVEN

Hazel halted at the sight of Duke ferociously pawing at a fresh-dug grave under the thick Douglas fir branches. Her mouth dried as she contemplated what lay beneath the soil. The length measured about the size of her eight-year-old son. *No, it can't be him.* Wouldn't a mother know if her son had perished? Feel it somehow? Hazel had to see. She took a step, but Mitchell stopped her approach.

"Let Duke do his job." Mitchell draped his arm around her waist, offering her comfort, as if he knew exactly what she was thinking.

A gust of wind rustled the corner of a piece of fabric beside where the dog dug before lifting and twirling it toward them like tumbleweed rolling through an Old Western movie setting. The object caught on a group of weeds inches away from where Hazel stood.

Jackson's superhero bandana.

"No!" Hazel dropped to her knees and buried her head in her hands.

Mitchell kneeled on one side of her, Bree on the other.

Their unified front to offer support.

Voices buzzed around her in a tunnel-like manner. Loud, but unrecognizable. Her father's barked command for searchers to dig barely recorded in her brain. *My baby is gone. Lord, why? Why?* This couldn't be happening.

She registered a hand resting on her back. Whispered words of comfort on both sides. She willed them away. Willed them not to be true. Her son was not dead. Words caught in her throat. She had to tell them to dig faster—she had to know—but her mind wouldn't allow her to utter a sentence.

Duke ceased barking.

Smoke assaulted her nose, and she coughed.

Shouts sounded.

Fingers snapped in front of her face. "Hazel! Come out of it." Her father's growled words muffled nearby.

Someone grabbed her shoulders, shaking her, yelling at her. "It's not Jackson!"

The words finally registered.

She shot to her feet as the scene before her came into focus and her ears cleared.

"Pumpkin, it's a stuffed teddy bear," her father said. "Not Jackson."

Her father's use of her nickname brought her out of the trance that had held her captive for an unknown amount of time. It had felt like an eternity.

Hazel's hand flew to her mouth and tears of relief stumbled down her face. *Thank You, God.*

Mitchell brought her into an embrace.

She let him comfort her and lingered in his arms. "Not him?"

"No, Hazel. We'll find him," Bree said.

Mitchell released his hold on her, but held her at arm's length. "She's right. We will."

Their gazes locked. What did she see in his eyes?

Bree cleared her throat, breaking the moment, and Hazel's unspoken question remained unanswered.

"I found something!" Nora yelled nearby.

"What is it?" Hazel dashed toward her coworker.

Nora pointed to a broken bracelet stuck in the dirt beside the large teddy bear.

Hazel fingered the matching one on her wrist and inhaled sharply. "That's Jackson's." She held out her arm. "He made us both one a year ago. We promised each other we wouldn't take them off. A bonding pact we made after some boys had bullied him in school." Her gaze shifted to her father's. "Dad, someone must have torn it off, along with his bandana. Firebug has him." Fresh tears flowed.

"You're wrong, Hazel." Supervisor Frank Hoyt crossed his arms—the earlier gentle father gone. "I refuse to believe that. The boys are just lost somewhere. The bracelet and bandana probably came off when they ran through the trees, then Firebug found them to use against you."

Hazel ignored her father and addressed Max. "Where did Duke find the bandana?"

The K-9 handler pointed to the tree. "Protruding from the grave."

"So the scent led your dog here," Hazel said, more to herself than anyone else. The situation became clearer in her foggy brain.

"Yes." Max squatted in front of his dog and offered him a treat for his reward.

"But why bury the bracelet and teddy bear together?" Bree asked.

Hazel straightened, a prickle crawling up her back like a creeping spider. She shuddered. "To lure us here."

Her friend grazed Hazel's arm. "For what?"

Mitchell shifted his stance. "To take his revenge."

His whispered words spoke volumes—and truth.

"He texted me earlier, warning me to get out of the wilderness or someone would die." He clutched Bree's upper arm. "We need to go before it's too late."

His sister wiggled out of his hold. "I'm not going any-where without Hazel."

"And I'm not leaving my son behind. I don't scare that easily." Hazel unsnapped her holster buckle and rested her hand on her sidearm.

Her father placed his large hand over Hazel's, stopping her from withdrawing her gun. "Easy now. This could just all be a ploy and he's simply toying with us."

Hazel freed herself and stepped away from her father. "You don't think I know that? That's all Firebug has been doing. But why? Why me? Why does he want Jackson so badly? He's an innocent child and doesn't deserve to be hunted in the wilderness!"

Her father grabbed Hazel's shoulders. "I. Don't. Know." He paused. "You've got to keep a level head, Warden Hoyt. Treat this like any other lost person in our park."

How could her father stay so calm when his grandson was in danger?

Mitchell placed his hand on her father's arm. "Sir, I mean no disrespect, but don't be so hard on her. She's doing her best to bring her son—your Bear Cub—home."

Her father poked Mitchell in the chest. "You stay out of this. It's not your concern."

Mitchell stood eye to eye with Hazel's father. "Really? I've almost drowned, been barricaded in a burning cabin, saved your barn and horses, and gotten shot to help find Jackson. I think I've proven myself."

Bree tugged on her brother's hand. "Mitchell, stand—"

Hazel positioned herself between them. "Stop! All of you. This is what Firebug wants. To divide us, so we'll let our guard down." She eyed her father, then Mitchell. "I will not allow that to happen. For Jackson and those boys. We remain a united front. You hear me?" Her voice carried beyond their area. "The boys need us working together."

"I agree," Nora said. "Let's do this and find those boys."

Hazel silenced the insecurities threatening to explode in front of the group. *God, I need You. Now. Keep us unified as a family, trying to save the boys.*

She addressed the team. "Let's talk about the information we have. We don't know if Firebug has captured the boys. Jackson may have dropped these objects on purpose. I trained him to give me bread crumbs if he was ever lost. Firebug probably found them and is now using them against us. Against me." She pushed down doubts bubbling to the surface and caught her father's gaze. "I refuse to believe anything else, but you're right. We treat this as we would any other search." Hard as that would be for her, she realized her father was correct. This time. She had to curb her emotions and keep them in check, or her father would probably cut her from the team.

Even when it was her son out there. Alone.

Hazel inspected the small clearing just off the path, secluded from a popular hiking trail. "Okay, he picked this spot for a reason. He's out there, watching. Waiting to pounce like a hungry lion. We fight him—together."

Her radio squawked.

"Mama—we're—"

Hazel sucked in a breath and yanked her radio off her shoulder. "Jackson? Where are you?"

Her son was alive.

Hope surged throughout Hazel's body as the sun peeked out from under a cloud.

Mitchell's pulse pounded as his gaze met Hazel's widened eyes.

"Jackson, are you okay?" She yelled into the radio.

"Yes—with Teddy and Elijah—took Stan's radio." His broken words told Mitchell they were in a remote area.

Hazel smiled at her son's message. "That's okay. Tell me where you are."

"Hiding—cave—"

"Jackson! What cave?" Hazel's tone raised a pitch as alarm flashed on her pretty face.

Silence answered.

"Jackson?"

Nothing.

"Bear Cub, come again!" Frank's voice cracked, exposing the emotion he'd demanded Hazel contain earlier.

The radio waves remained silent.

Hazel's forehead crinkled as defeat was once again displayed on her forlorn expression.

Mitchell rubbed her back. "He's safe, Hazel. Firebug doesn't have them."

Her eyes narrowed. "What makes you say that?"

"Because he said they were hiding. That's a good sign, right?" He reached to move a stray strand out of her eyes, then dropped his hand.

Not here, Mitch. You're not alone.

"He's right, Hazel. And he has a radio. He could call again." Bree walked between them, nudging him away from her best friend. His sister turned her gaze to him.

Her glaring eyes told him one thing.

Stay away from my friend.

"But why didn't he call earlier?" Hazel asked.

"Maybe they were out of range or something." Frank pulled out his map and gestured his daughter to a nearby picnic table. "Let's rethink our search and look at all known caves." He sat and spread out the map.

Hazel hesitated.

Frank glanced over his shoulder. "Come on, Hazel. Now! We have lots of ground to cover."

She lurched into motion and sat across from her father.

"Mitch, I need to talk to you." Bree's whispered words spoke volumes. She walked to the edge of the clearing, beckoning him to follow.

She was upset with him for some strange reason.

Great. This was all he needed right now. An angry sister.

He followed. "What's wrong, Bree?"

She placed her fisted hands on her hips. "Stop crushing on Hazel."

Where did that come from? "What? I'm not." *Liar. You are.* He suppressed his thoughts, as he wouldn't admit that to his sister.

Bree poked his chest. "You are. I see the way you look at her. Stay away."

"We're just friends." Heat surged and sat on the edge of his emotions. "Don't tell me what to do. You've done that too much lately."

"Oh, we're on this topic again. I did not demand you speak at Mom's funeral."

Mitchell threw his hands in the air. "Sis, I don't want to fight. It's neither the time nor the place."

She tilted her head. "You brought it up and we have to talk about it someday. Mitch, I want you back in my life. I've missed you. This past year has been hard. Losing Mom, and then you too."

"Bree, the crack in our relationship started with Ivy, not when Mom died." Why couldn't Mitchell let it go? He longed for a stronger bond between them.

His sister let out an extended, audible sigh. "How many times do I have to say I'm sorry? She was trouble, and I wanted to warn you. Girls know these things, bro."

Mitchell massaged the knot in his shoulder. She was right, but how could he admit his failure? He'd also seen some signs, but by the time he broke it off, Ivy had gone full-fledged obsessive. A mistake that nearly cost his life.

"Bro, when are you going to come back to God?" she asked.

That was the other fight they'd had many times. But how could Mitchell trust in a God who allowed so much pain in his life?

Mitchell shook his head. "Bree, not now. We need to help Hazel."

"Well, then, if you want to help her, stay away from her. Hazel's been through too much for you to break her heart."

"I told you, we're only friends, and that's all we'll ever be. She's your best friend and like a sister to me." Words from a childhood song played in the back of his mind. *Liar, liar...pants on fire.*

A branch crunched behind him. Mitchell pivoted and saw Hazel. Her expression turned into a scowl.

Great. She'd just heard him say he only thought of her as a sister. Definitely not the truth. *Now you've gone and done it. Stupid, Mitch!*

Perhaps it was for the best. He couldn't deal with more heartache.

Hazel lowered her head and pointed to where her father sat. "We have a plan of attack."

"Good," Bree said. "I'm going to use the toilet. There's one close, isn't there?"

"Yes, a vault toilet at the trailhead." Hazel pointed.

"Okay, I'll be right back." Bree jogged toward the path.

Mitchell stepped forward. "Listen, I'm sorry you heard—"

Hazel inched backward. "I don't have time for this. I need to find my son. You can either leave or help. Your choice." She hustled over to the picnic table.

Ouch. But how could he blame her? She never should have heard his comment.

He never should have said it, especially when he knew in his heart it wasn't true. He did indeed have romantic feelings for his little sister's best friend.

Well, one thing was for sure. He wasn't about to abandon her now. Even if she didn't want him around. He would not disappoint Hazel Hoyt.

He squared his shoulders and walked to the picnic table, determination to find her son taking over.

Mitchell sat beside her and ignored her tightened expression. "Tell me the plan."

Over the next fifteen minutes, Frank explained how they would split up all the known caves among the search teams. Even though they'd already cleared some of them, they realized the boys were probably moving around.

Frank stood. "I'll assign each of the teams." He pointed. "You, Bree and Mitchell take this one."

Hazel pushed herself upright. "Speaking of Bree, where is she? She should be back by now."

"You're right," Mitchell said. "I'll go—"

A bloodcurdling scream pierced the afternoon hour.

Bree.

Mitchell bolted toward his sister's desperate cry.

Lord, don't take her too.

TWELVE

"Bree! Where are you?" Mitchell yelled as he raced toward the park toilets. Her last known location. *Please be okay, my sweet sister.* Remorse over his harshness toward her tortured his mind. What-ifs hounded him with each step he took, as if mocking him. What if he'd been a better brother? Would they be in this predicament? What if she dies and he couldn't tell her he was sorry? If he'd only left the wilderness, perhaps she'd be okay.

"Bree, where are you?" Hazel's cry and pounding footfalls behind him told him she had followed.

They both stopped in front of the tiny vault toilet. Mitchell turned to Hazel. "Can you check?"

She nodded and entered.

He waited outside and yelled his sister's name.

No response.

Hazel exited and shook her head.

Mitchell's cell phone dinged, and he checked his texts.

This is what you get for not leaving. Firebug

A picture of Bree lying motionless on a ledge appeared on his screen.

"No!" Mitchell staggered backward, thumping against the building. He slid down the wall until he rested on the ground. "This is all my fault." Two years of pent-up emotion exploded, and the tears flowed. He wasn't one to show his feelings in public, but he couldn't contain his grief. *Why, God?*

"What is it?" Hazel squatted in front of him.

"He got to Bree." Mitchell held out his phone to Hazel, showing the picture.

"No!" she yelled.

He hung his head. "She's dead because of me."

Hazel popped to her feet. "We don't know that. That ledge isn't far from here." She unhooked her radio. "Dad, grab the rope gear and meet us at Fireweed Cliff. Call SAR and get the medics there. Bree is hurt, and we must get to her right away."

"Copy that. See you there." Frank Hoyt's breathless last sentence revealed he was running.

"Mitch, I know you're hurting, but we need to get to this ridge. Right now." Hazel bent down and helped him up. "I refuse to believe she's gone. Come on."

Mitchell snapped to attention and nodded. The pair ran down the trail toward the cliff.

Five minutes later, Mitchell examined the picture one more time before scanning the area. "Over there." He pointed.

"Why do you think that?" Hazel asked.

He enlarged the frame. "Look at these succulents. They're not along the ridge where we're standing, but they're there." Mitchell stopped at the location where he guessed Firebug had taken the picture. Yellow flowers had sprouted from the succulents nestled among a rock formation at the cliff's edge. Mitchell glanced over the side. "Bree! Where are you?"

His sister lay unmoving on a ledge beneath him, precariously close to the edge. He turned back to Hazel. "There she is!" He cupped his hands around his mouth. "Bree! Can you hear me?"

"Bree!" Hazel yelled. "Talk to us."

Silence.

Mitchell stumbled backward.

Hazel shouted his sister's name again.

It was no use. Bree was gone. She couldn't have survived the drop. Mitchell sank to his knees and looked upward. "Why, God? Why did you take her too?"

Hazel brought him into her arms. "I'm so sorry. I'm—"

A faint cry sounded below.

Mitchell drew in a sharp breath and shot upward. "Bree?" He peeked over the side.

His sister stirred.

"She's alive!" Mitchell yelled. "Bree, we're here. Help is coming."

She moved her arms and tried to sit up.

"No, Bree. Stay still." He had to keep her calm, because if she moved much more, she'd fall to her death. "Take deep breaths."

Hazel unhooked her radio. "Dad, we found her. We're just down from where the cliff trails meet. Where are you?"

"Approaching the bend in the path," he said.

"Hurry!" Hazel looked around. "We have to figure out where to anchor a line. I'm going down."

Mitchell grabbed her arm. "No, you're not. Your side isn't strong enough. I'll go."

She crossed her arms. "And you are?"

"Neither of you are going." Frank approached quickly. "I am. I've done many rescues in my day."

Her father appeared with Nora and a couple of rescue workers.

Hazel shook her head. "No, Dad. Let someone younger do it."

Mitchell studied the man. Even though he was in his late fifties, Frank Hoyt's buffed muscles revealed a regimented workout routine. The fit park supervisor would have no problems scaling the cliff wall. "Hazel, he'll be fine."

"Thank you for the vote of confidence," Frank said, then eyed his daughter. "At least someone thinks I'm capable."

Hazel frowned. "Sorry. Just worried about you."

"I've got this." Frank turned to the rescue workers. "Secure two lines. Nora, help me into the harness."

As the team worked at getting Frank suited up to make the treacherous trek down the mountain to rescue Bree, he called down to her. "Are you hurt?"

"Just scrapes and bruises, I think. The branches cushioned my fall."

Mitchell addressed Frank. "You check her out. If she's not strong enough, we'll have to get a chopper here. When are the medics coming?"

"They're out with the SAR chopper right now, but Evan and Vanessa should be here soon. They've been informed of what we're dealing with here." Frank picked up a second harness. "Hazel, hook this up to me. We'll bring her up separately if she's able. We've got to hurry and get her up before the fires worsen. We may have to evacuate the park."

"Mitchell, have you had an update from your team?" Hazel asked.

"You guys get ready to save Bree. I'll call in and check." He unhooked his radio and pressed the button. "Princess, you there?" He waited. "Can you give me an update?"

"It's not looking good," Princess said. "Our choppers are dropping water from their buckets near the hot spot."

"I can smell smoke. We're at Fireweed Cliff. How close is the fire?"

"North of your location."

"Any contact from Smokey?" Mitchell asked.

"Nothing. Morgan is out searching. I don't like it. It's not like him to leave a job unfinished."

Mitchell noted the worry in her voice. "Okay, give me regular updates."

"Will do. Stay safe."

"You too." He clicked off and walked back to the group. "Wildfire is getting closer. Let's get Bree up quickly. I don't want to take any risks."

"Understood," Frank said. "Let's do this."

The team secured Frank's line, and he proceeded over the edge.

Mitchell held his breath as the man placed one foot gingerly onto a crevice in the rock wall, followed by the other.

Tumbling rocks clanged against the cliff, followed by Frank's cry.

"Dad! Be careful." Hazel's distraught tone revealed her uneasiness.

Frank's foot slipped, sending a large rock toward Bree.

"Bree, cover yourself!" Mitchell yelled.

The rock tumbled to the right, barely missing his sister. Mitchell blew out the breath he'd been holding. "Come on, we need to get her up here."

"Dad's going as fast as he can, Mitchell." Hazel's eyes narrowed. "The wall took a lot of rain damage in yesterday's storm. He has to take it slowly. You don't want more rocks tumbling on top of Bree, and neither do I."

She spoke the truth, but Mitchell's impatient streak wanted his sister rescued now before she suffered even more injuries. Plus he had to tell her he was sorry for how he had failed in their relationship. It was time to put it to rest.

Mitchell also didn't miss the tone in Hazel's voice. The closeness he felt yesterday had disappeared after she'd heard his comment about only wanting to be friends. Why had Mitchell been so stupid to say such a thing when he knew in his heart it was wrong? He did have feelings for her...even after only two days.

Movement sounded behind him, and he turned.

Evan and Vanessa jogged down the path, carrying their medical equipment and rescue basket.

"Where's your sister?" Evan asked.

Mitchell pointed over the cliff. "Frank is working his way down to her."

"Any known injuries?" Vanessa asked.

"Nothing serious that we know of," Mitchell said.

Evan looked down. "That's quite a drop. It's amazing she's still alive. We need to get her to the hospital fast. I'm concerned she could have internal bleeding from that fall."

"Dad has reached her!" Hazel yelled. "He's checking her over."

Moments later, Frank helped Bree stand. He then gave them the thumbs-up. "Only scrapes and a bump on her head. I'm gearing her up now."

After Frank added the clip to Bree's harness, he tugged on the line. "Ready!" Slowly, the team maneuvered Bree to the top, with Frank beside her all the way.

Vanessa and Evan helped her into the rescue basket and checked her vitals.

"Pulse is strong." Evan examined her head. "I don't like that bump. We'll get you checked out thoroughly."

Hazel stepped to her side. "Tell us what happened. How did Firebug get to you?"

Bree breathed in and out slowly. "I went to the toilet and when I came out, two rough hands grabbed me from be-hind. He dragged me here and said, 'This is the price your brother has to pay for not obeying me.' Then he pushed me. I grabbed on to some shrubbery and it helped break my fall. Thank God for that ledge."

Mitchell clung to her side, hovering. "Bree, I'm so sorry. This is all my fault. I should have listened to Firebug."

"Please don't think that," Bree said. "This is *his* fault. No one else's."

"I almost lost you and I have so much I want to say to you." Mitchell's shoulders slumped. "I've been a terrible brother, and I'm sorry for how I've treated you. You tried to warn me about Ivy, and I wouldn't believe you." He didn't miss Hazel's raised brow. Great, now she'd question him. He addressed his sister. "I'm sorry for not being there when Mom died. I was a lousy brother, but all that is going to change now."

Bree smiled. "Mitch, it's in the past. I'm sorry for pushing. I know now you were hurting too. Let's move on. I need to ask you one thing."

"Anything."

"Come back to God. He's waiting."

Mitchell pursed his lips. Could he?

His cell phone dinged, halting their conversation. He retrieved his phone and swiped the screen.

I underestimated your sister. Next time she dies. Get out of my forest. Firebug

A lump clogged Mitchell's throat. He had to protect his sister at all costs and if that meant leaving the wilderness and risking losing his job...so be it.

Hazel didn't miss the pain on Mitchell's handsome face, but was it more from whatever text he'd received or his conversation with Bree? Hazel hated to intrude on their intimate moment, but Mitchell obviously had to get whatever he needed to say out in the open. And who was Ivy? Why did the name of another woman coil Hazel's gut? It wasn't like he wanted anything more from their relationship. *She's your best friend and like a sister to me.* Mitchell's confession to Bree echoed in Hazel's mind. He would only ever see her as a little sister.

Move on, Hazel. You have more important issues...like finding your son.

She nudged Mitchell to the side. "What is it?"

He raised his cell phone in her direction. "Firebug again. I need to leave the park. Bree's life is at risk."

Hazel's jaw dropped before searching in all directions. "He's close and knows Bree didn't die. We need to get her a police escort."

"I agree, but who can we trust?"

"Dad has a ton of connections on the force. Let's check with him."

They approached her father.

"Dad, Firebug specifically targeted Bree and we need to get her police protection." Hazel unbuckled her father's harness.

"How do you know that?" he asked as he took off his climbing gear.

Mitchell raised his phone. "Because he's been texting me threats."

Her father read the screen and scowled. "Okay, I'll contact Stein."

Hazel helped him stuff the gear into a large duffle bag. "Firebug seems to have eyes and ears everywhere. Can we trust Stein and his team, Dad?"

"Yes. He saved my life years ago, remember?" He unfastened his radio. "I'll get right on it." He walked away.

"Let's tell Bree."

"I know we have to, but I don't want her to get scared."

Mitchell walked back to his sister's side. "How are you doing?"

"Evan is taking good care of me," Bree said. "We're heading to the hospital now."

Hazel patted her hand. "I'm so glad you're okay. I don't know what I'd do if I lost you too." Her voice quivered.

Stay strong, Hazel. Jackson needs you.

"You'll find the boys, sweet friend," Bree said. "God's got this."

Did He? It didn't feel that way. Hazel had completely believed God was in control, but certain events in her life had chipped away at her rock-solid faith.

"Bree, we have to tell you something important." Mitchell leaned in and kissed his sister's cheek. "You'll be getting a police escort and I'm coming along too. I didn't listen to Firebug before, so I can't stay in the park or he will try to kill you again."

Bree frowned. "No! Stay with Hazel. Find Jackson and those boys. They're more important right now. I'll be fine."

Leave it to Bree to put others in front of her own safety. It was in her DNA and why she sacrificed her time to go on mission trips.

"I can't risk your life," Mitchell said.

"Well, I can't let you risk Hazel's and those boys' lives either. Plus you need to catch Firebug and stop these wildfires. Evan, let's go."

Hazel didn't miss the emotion in her friend's quivering voice. She didn't want to leave but she also wouldn't let Mitchell abandon his duty to end the turmoil Firebug created across the wilderness.

Mitchell let out a ragged moan as his shoulders hunched forward. "Nothing like ordering your big brother around, little sis."

"Someone has to." She gave him a weak smile. "Find those boys. Love you."

Once again, Mitchell kissed his sister's cheek. "Love you more."

Hazel's dad approached the group. "Constable Porter will meet you at the fork in the trail and escort you out. Stein will post a guard at the hospital, Bree." He turned to Hazel. "I'm going to get a search update." He walked away.

"Time to go." Evan lifted one end of the basket and Vanessa the other.

Bree waved as they reached the bend in the path.

Mitchell stood still, watching them, as if frozen in place.

Hazel stroked his arm. "She's in good hands."

He rubbed his eye before addressing her. "I know. I just can't believe I almost lost my sister to this maniac." He squared his shoulders. "This ends. Now. He's going down."

While she appreciated his determination to catch Firebug, they must tread carefully. She wouldn't allow anyone to put her son at risk. "I understand, but we can't do anything rash."

He placed his hands on his hips. "You don't think I realize that? I'm not the careless teenager from years ago. I've grown up, Hazel."

Like she hadn't seen his maturity. The man before her impressed her, but she had to be sure he wouldn't take any chances with her son's life.

She also didn't miss the irritation in his voice.

Hazel fisted her hands at her side. Since when had she become her father? Had she just gotten a glimpse of what life was like for him with eight children? Did his protective nature cause him to be so hard on them?

While she caught a peek into what caused his totalitarian nature, she refused to be that person. *Hazel, you're better than that.* She bristled and, in that moment, chose to show kindness instead of harshness. She suppressed the anger bubbling inside. "I'm sorry. You're right. You almost lost your sister. I get it."

His expression softened. "Listen, what I said earlier about—"

Hazel's radio sputtered to life. "Mama, help! We're— ridge—hurt—"

She gasped and pressed the Talk button. "Jackson! Say again."

Silence greeted her.

She pushed the button again. "Jackson! Where are you?"

"—more—find—" The radio squealed before completely cutting out.

Relief washed over her at the sound of her son's voice, followed by a surge of terror.

She had to save her son.

Now.

THIRTEEN

Mitchell caught the alarm in Jackson's voice as he tried to relay their location to his mother, but all that came through the radio airwaves were broken words. Hazel stood frozen, her horror-struck eyes staring straight ahead. He squeezed her hand, hoping to give her some type of reassurance he was there for her. "We'll find them. I caught the word *ridge*."

His voice jarred her into action, and she removed her paper map, rushing over to a nearby picnic table. "The park has many ridges." She spread out the map and sat.

He plunked down across from her with thoughts of his sister heavy on his mind. *Lord, if You're listening, protect Bree and help her be okay. I can't lose her like I lost Mom and Dad. She's all I have left.*

Frank sprinted toward them and settled beside his daughter. "I heard Jackson's radio call. Where do you think his location is? I want your opinion."

Hazel jerked her head up from studying the map.

Her father's question and comment obviously surprised Hazel. Had this horrendous day given them all a proverbial kick in the pants? A shake in the direction toward reconciliation with their family members? Bree's words filled Mitchell's mind. *Come back to God. He's waiting.*

Was that true? A reconciliation with Him too? He wasn't

sure. Could he trust in the One who stole his parents from him and allowed Ivy to take a revenge that had thrust him into a deep pit?

Forgive.

Why had the word tumbled into his thoughts? He could hear his mother telling him to put the past where it belonged—in the past—and move on. *Forgive those who have wronged you.* Her words. But what if that was God?

"Mitchell, what are your thoughts?" Hazel asked.

Her question transported him back to the present, and he shoved thoughts about God to the back of his mind. More pressing issues demanded his attention. He straightened. "Sorry, what did you say?"

Hazel pointed to different ridges on the map. "Dad thinks this ridge, but what about these?"

Mitchell leaned closer and examined the Micmore wilderness. One ridge drew his eye.

The ridge they never wanted a child to wander toward. He glanced back at Hazel. Dare he admit his thoughts?

He exhaled and pointed. "I hate to say it, but this one seems right, based on where we know they've been."

Hazel's eyes widened.

And he knew why.

Micmore Ridge was the most dangerous area in her park and she knew it.

But it made the most sense with the words Jackson sputtered and where they'd been.

Frank flew off the picnic bench and paced around the table and over to the tree line. "No! They can't be there. It's too far north and Jackson knows to stay away from the area."

Hazel expelled a long breath before bringing out a marker from her vest pocket. "He's right, Dad." She circled different spots on the map. "They probably traveled in this direction from the river and cabin. Plus Jackson said the words *ridge* and *more*. Micmore Ridge." She circled the location.

Frank stomped back to the table and placed his finger on a ridge closer to where the wildfire blazed. Close to where Duke had uncovered Jackson's bandana. Where Bree was pushed. "What about here?"

Mitchell crossed his arms and shook his head. "No. I feel that was a diversion to trick us into thinking that's where the boys are. Firebug is smart. He's—" Mitchell sucked in a breath. "That's why he started the fire there. Hazel, this tells me he knows where the boys are and he's trying to keep us away from them."

She shot to her feet. "Dad, call in Sami. Get her to fly her SAR chopper over the ridge and investigate. See if the boys are there. Then we can move in."

The ridge was only accessible via helicopter.

"On it." Frank unholstered his radio and hurried away.

Hazel plopped down on the picnic bench and held her head in her hands, leaning on her legs. "I need to save my son."

Mitchell sat beside her and rubbed her back. "We'll find him."

She looked up.

His gaze met hers and locked.

She stiffened.

His eyes fell to her lips. What would it be like to kiss her? He inched closer, holding his breath.

Then stopped. *Mitch, remember Ivy.*

But Hazel wasn't Ivy.

His heart knew that, but his head didn't agree.

He cleared his throat and stood. "I need to check in with Princess."

And step away from you before my heart sinks further.

Two things he now knew for sure…

He was falling for his little sister's best friend.

And he had to guard his emotions because he couldn't take the heartache again.

Hazel fiddled with her park warden vest as she waited for word from Sami. Her father had reported the chopper had left and now circled the area. *Come on, Sami. Find the boys.* Hazel reflected back to the scene with Mitchell earlier. Was he about to kiss her? His actions certainly had leaned in that direction, but then he'd jerked away. Had he realized he only saw her as a little sister? Was that why he'd been so hot and cold?

It's for the best, Hazel. Your track record and trust in men is faulty.

Mitchell sat next to her, listening to updates from his team on his two-way radio. They had reported the fires were getting closer. They had slowed them down, but the relentless Rocky Mountain Firebug hadn't helped when he set additional small fires in the area.

"Hazel!" Her father raced down the path. "Sami reported they found Teddy hovering on a ledge. They tried to rescue him, but he refused to budge. He wants you."

She popped off the bench and winced, holding her side. "He's Jackson's best friend, and I know his personality. Teddy is skittish and probably terrified. He trusts me. Let's go."

He grabbed her shoulder. "You're wounded, remember? You rappel down that cliff and you risk not only your life but Teddy's."

"He's right," Mitchell said. "It's too dangerous on that ridge."

"I'm fine." No way would she let her father talk her out of saving the boy's life.

Not today.

Pain or no pain.

"Let's get to the chopper pad." She hustled down the path, not waiting for rebukes from her father or the man who only wanted to be a friend.

You've got this.

Forty-five minutes later, Hazel peered out the helicopter's window, staring at the smoke rising in the distance as she listened to base camp chatter over the radio through her headset. It was now midafternoon, and she sat in the chopper with Mitchell, Sami, the pilot, and Hank, a search-and-rescue worker.

Her father had remained behind to redirect the search parties. They wanted to get in as much hunting as possible before they lost daylight. Hazel had suited up with full rescue gear, biting her lip as anxiety over getting Teddy off the ledge safely traumatized her. *Get it together.*

"Mitchell, I have Carey Morgan wanting to talk to you," Sami said through the headset. "I'm patching him into our coms."

"Boomer, report." Carey's voice blared in their ears.

Mitchell covered his mouthpiece and hissed out a breath. "Great. My boss," he whispered. He removed his hand and spoke into the coms. "Boomer here. What's up, Morgan?"

"Princess reported you're helping SAR? Why am I not hearing this from you? You promised regular updates." His deafening voice revealed the man's anger.

"I tried to call you, but was told you were not to be disturbed."

"Well, I would appreciate better updates or I will bench you."

Hazel tensed at the man's harsh words. Carey Morgan would not get in her way of finding the boys. She didn't have time for the politics happening with this leader. "Sir, this is park warden Hazel Hoyt. We require Mitchell's help with a special rescue mission. We're concerned there are fires in the region and need his expertise."

Mitchell tilted his head.

She shrugged. It was kind of true. She needed his knowledge. "So, if you have questions, please take it up with Supervisor Frank Hoyt."

"Understood. I certainly don't want to suffer that man's wrath." A pause. "Now, can I speak to my employee, Warden Hoyt?"

She suppressed the urge to laugh out loud and gestured for Mitchell to go ahead.

He winked as a smile played on his lips.

Lips she definitely wanted to kiss.

She looked away to hide the pain from his earlier rejection. Pain she knew settled on her face.

"Go ahead, Morgan. Anything further on Smokey?" Mitchell asked.

"I have team members checking out his favorite hangouts, but it's not like him to leave midway through a shift."

"Agreed. Princess has a good control on the team. She knows what she's doing."

Silence paused the airwaves. "Actually, I'm going to come too. I think I want to be hands-on for this one. I'll update you more on the fire later. Morgan out."

Hazel turned her gaze back to Mitchell.

He rubbed the bridge of his nose. "Great, now I have my leader hovering. He's been watching me like a hawk."

She studied his handsome face.

Stop it, Hazel. Concentrate.

"Why do you feel that is?" she asked.

"Randy Jacobs recommended me for the team leader position, and Morgan seems to resent me for it. I'm thinking Randy pushed him into giving it to me over Smokey."

Mitchell tapped his thumb on the armrest. "From what I can tell, Smokey can do no wrong in Morgan's eyes."

"You said earlier you moved back because you missed the mountains. What about Bree?"

His gaze snapped to hers.

Oops. From his expression, she guessed she'd just walked into the no-fly zone of relationship talk. "Sorry. None of my business. I just know how much she missed you."

He leaned against the headrest. "It's okay. I have lots of regrets when it comes to our relationship, but we took a step in the right direction today."

She patted his hand. "I'm glad. I know your father's death when you were teenagers was hard. Then losing your mother threw you both a curveball."

"She was my best friend."

Hazel didn't miss the emotion in his words. She remembered their close connection. He'd definitely been a Mama's boy, but in a good way.

"Who's Ivy?" Hazel blurted out the question before she could stop it, but she wanted to know.

He averted his gaze.

But not before she caught an odd expression on his face. Terror?

What in the world?

"I'd rather not talk about her," he whispered.

"Folks, we're on approach," Sami said from her cockpit.

Their arrival at Micmore Ridge was probably just as well. She'd just entered a territory he obviously didn't want to talk about.

Hazel lifted her binoculars. "Keep your eyes peeled for the other boys." She scanned the area. Through a clearing in the wilderness she spied an abandoned park station and lookout. Built years ago, the buildings were now too remote for their team. The ridge itself was only accessible via helicopter, but the station could be reached on horseback.

She continued to study the area, searching for signs of the boys. The chopper crested over the mountain to the other side. Movement caught her eye, and she focused in on a ledge jutting out from the cliff overlooking a vast mountain region. "I see Teddy. Time to get ready."

The boy sat with his legs to his chest, huddled close to the wall.

Mixed emotions toyed with Hazel. Relief that it wasn't her son sitting on a dangerous ledge, but worry that Jackson was still out there somewhere. If it had been him, she could have saved her son and tucked him safely in his own bed tonight. She threw up a silent prayer that would still happen.

"Hazel, we're losing our window of opportunity here," Sami said into the coms. "We need to get in and get out quickly. High winds are moving in."

Not good.

"Got it." Hazel double-checked her buckles. She ensured her medical pouch was secure. First aid was a requirement for all wardens, with regular refresher courses.

Hank stood and handed her another harness. "An extra one for Teddy, but first check his injuries and then we can determine the method to bring him up."

She did as he said and silently went through the safety checks in her head, triple-checking as she moved to the door.

Hank added the clip and hooked her to the rappel line. "Communicate with us constantly."

"Got it." She adjusted her coms. "You hear me okay?"

Hank nodded. "It really should be me going down there, not you. However, he went hysterical when we tried. Put us and him in danger."

"Sorry about that. Teddy knows me."

He tightened his lips. "I hope you're not crusty like your old man."

Where had that come from? She suppressed a chuckle. Sad her father had that reputation. Well, she would not become her father's daughter—so to speak.

"She's not." Mitchell caught her gaze. "You've got this. I have total faith in you."

Thankful for his encouragement, she smiled and positioned herself in front of the chopper's door.

"Approaching the drop zone," Sami said. "ETA, one minute."

"You ready?" Hank asked.

She checked her gear one more time before nodding.

He opened the door, and she placed herself in the correct stance, waiting for the all-clear signal from Sami.

"Hazel, we're ready," the pilot said.

She took a breath and gave Hank the thumbs-up sign. He hit the button for the line to rappel.

She pushed off the helicopter and slowly descended the fifty plus feet toward Teddy. When she reached the ledge, she pulled on the rope to give herself more slack.

Teddy scrambled backward, cowering against the mountain wall.

He didn't realize it was her. Terror flashed in his widened eyes.

She took off her helmet. "Teddy, it's me. Jackson's Mom. Like you asked."

He inched toward her as tears trickled down his face.

She kneeled in front of him and embraced him. "I've got you, buddy."

He hiccuped in between sobs.

"Are you hurt?" Hazel held up her hands. "I'm going to check you to be safe. Is that okay?"

He nodded.

She gently examined his legs for injuries as she eyed him. No pain registered in his eyes. Good. She shifted to his arms.

He cried when she reached his left elbow area.

"That hurts?"

Once again, he nodded.

She finished her examination with no further pain points. Hazel placed herself at his eye level. "Teddy, you're okay. Looks like it's just your arm that's hurt. I'm going to put you into a harness, so we can go for a fun ride up into the chopper." She pointed upward.

His eyes followed her finger, then widened.

"Don't worry. You'll be safe with me." Hazel retrieved a sling from her medical pouch. "I'm going to put your arm into this, okay? Can you stand? Stay close to the wall, though."

She had to keep him calm. If he panicked, they both might slip.

A huge raindrop spattered on the ledge.

She gazed at the clouds. Not good. She had to move fast. She jerked her head back. Vertigo hit her and she swayed. *Big breaths, Hazel.* She inhaled and exhaled, waiting for the elevator-like sensation to steady.

Seconds later, it passed and she carefully put the sling on Teddy, then prepared the harness. She put on her helmet. "Teddy may have a sprained arm," she said into her mouthpiece. "Hooking him up now."

"You're doing great, Hazel." Mitchell's voice sounded in her ear.

A sound she'd love to hear more often.

She pushed the thought aside and fastened the harness on Teddy, hooking him to hers. "Okay, big-bear-hug time."

He bit his lip.

"You've got this, Teddy. Just think of this as one of your roller-coaster rides. It's gonna be fun." At least she prayed it would be. She turned him around and placed her arms around his waist, bringing him close to her but being careful not to hurt his arm. "Hank, ready. Bring us up."

"Copy that."

The line locked, and they were lifted into the air. The closer they got to the chopper, the more her heart rate slowed.

Almost there.

A gust of wind whipped them to the right.

No! Hazel clutched Jackson's best friend closer.

Lord, keep us safe.

She held her breath and willed the swinging line to still.

FOURTEEN

Mitchell braced himself as the wind gusts shook the helicopter. He hated to fly but had insisted on coming with the team. He pursed his lips and waited for a glimpse of Hazel. *Hurry!*

A few seconds later, the top of her helmet appeared. Mitchell jumped up and moved to the opening, extending his arms to help bring them in.

The chopper continued to sway.

Hank and Mitchell each grabbed Hazel's arms and helped hoist the duo inside.

Hank closed the door. "Sami, get us out of here and radio the hospital. We'll land at their heliport."

"And contact Teddy's parents," Hazel said. "Have them meet us there. They'll want to see their son right away and be present while doctors examine him."

"Copy that," the pilot said.

Mitchell and Hank unfastened the harnesses and ropes, then buckled Teddy into a seat.

Mitchell tousled the boy's hair. "You're good, bud. Was your ride fun?"

Teddy remained silent.

Hazel sat beside her son's best friend. "This is Firefighter Mitchell. You can trust him and Hank."

"It was fun, but I don't want to do it again." Teddy leaned back in the seat.

"Mitchell, patching in your leader again." Sami's words were laced with irritation.

"Boomer, report," Morgan said.

Mitchell adjusted his mouthpiece. "Just rescued the boy. On our way to the hospital and then back to base camp. You at the wildfire EOC?"

"Yes. You guys best hurry. The fire has shifted directions with this wind and it's heading directly toward you. Will chat later."

Mitchell drew in a sharp breath. "Understood. Sami, what's our ETA?"

"Ten minutes. Maybe more in this wind."

At the mention of the wind, the chopper swayed.

Teddy screamed and Hazel drew him closer.

Mitchell had to help, but what could he do? He wasn't a father, let alone around children that often. An idea formed, and he leaned forward, bracing himself in case the chopper swayed again. "Teddy, can you tell us what happened on the ridge?"

Perhaps Mitchell could get Teddy's mind off the rocking helicopter.

"I don't remember."

Hazel rubbed his arm. "Think back. Did you slip and fall onto the ledge?"

His eyes widened like saucers. "No! He pushed me."

Hazel stared at Mitchell before addressing Teddy. "Who pushed you, sweetie?"

"The bad man in a mask."

So the boy hadn't seen his face. So much for an identification.

Mitchell required more information, but would Teddy remember anything else? "Why did he push you?"

"He wanted us to go with him. I tried to run, and he caught me. He called me a bad boy."

"Us? Where are Jackson and Elijah?" Hazel's hushed question was barely audible over the chopper's whomping blades.

"They took them." A fat tear rolled down his cheek. "I'm sorry. It's all my fault."

They?

Clearly, Firebug had an accomplice.

"Teddy, it's not your fault." Hazel wiped a tear from his face. "Who else was with the man?"

She'd caught the reference to a partner too.

"I don't know. She didn't tell me her name."

Mitchell whipped his gaze over to Hazel's, mouthing the word *she*?

Firebug was working with a woman?

"Did you see her face, son?" Mitchell asked.

Teddy's face twisted. "No. She had on dark glasses and a funny mask."

"What do you mean?" Hazel picked leaves from Teddy's tousled curls.

"It was white and looked like a bird's beak."

A K95 mask. Could it be someone involved in the medical field? Not necessarily.

Mitchell blew out a breath and sank back into his seat. "Do you know where they took Jackson and Elijah?"

He bit his lip and shook his head.

Hazel tucked him closer. "It's okay, Teddy. We'll find your friends. Did the man and woman say anything to each other? Could be a simple word or two."

The small eight-year-old tapped his index finger on his chin and clucked his tongue, as if thinking.

Mitchell suppressed a grin. He used to do the same

thing as a boy. Bree had called him a duckling because of it.

The boy's expression brightened. "Yes! She said 'I got Jackson for you, love' to the man."

So they were looking for a couple.

A question formed in Mitchell's head. "Teddy, did they say why they wanted Jackson?"

What was the reason they were targeting Hazel's son? She herself had asked the same question yesterday.

Teddy shook his head.

"Bud, were Jackson or Elijah hurt at all?" Hazel asked.

"No." Teddy looked into Hazel's face. "He left you bread crumbs. That's what Jackson said. What does that mean?"

Hazel smiled as her lip quivered. "He was helping me find you guys."

"He's smart."

"Can you tell us anything else, son?" Mitchell asked. "How did you escape the old cabin?"

Teddy straightened. "Mr. Stan helped us when the bad man came."

"What do you mean?" Hazel shifted in her seat.

"We were soaked from the rain and tired, so Jackson told us about the old cabin. The door was open, so we went in and found Snake." He puffed out a breath. "We were scared, but he made us some food to go with Jackson's granola bars and said he'd help us get back to the station. We were wet, so he went to get more firewood to warm us up. That was the last we saw of him before the bad man came."

"What happened next?" Mitchell clasped his hands together and leaned forward.

"The door burst open and the masked man came in. Said he would take us to our parents, but we didn't believe him." He turned to Hazel. "Jackson threw a bottle at him and hit him in the head."

Hazel smirked. "Good boy. How did you get out?"

"Stan came and fought with the man. He told us to run, so we did. Is Mr. Stan okay?"

Hazel's gaze met his. Tough question to answer.

She rubbed his arm. "Let's not worry about that right now. Where did you guys sleep last night?"

"In a cave." Teddy shivered. "It was cold and smelly."

Thankfully, the wildlife had stayed away from the boys. Bree would tell Mitchell that God had closed the cave to any roaring animals. Could Mitchell believe that?

"Son, why didn't you and the boys escape to the park station?" Hazel asked.

"Jackson tried to get us back there, but we kept going in circles. Then the bad men followed us and we hid." Teddy leaned against the seat and closed his eyes. Clearly he was done with the conversation.

Well, they at least had more information than they did thirty minutes ago, and one more boy was safe.

Two more to find.

"On approach, folks," Sami said into their headsets. "Ensure your seatbelts are fastened and tray tables are in the upright and locked position. It's gonna be a bumpy landing."

Under ordinary conditions Mitchell would have laughed at the pilot's quirky personality. But not today.

As the chopper lowered in altitude, Mitchell checked all their seatbelts, then looked out the window. The helicopter pad grew in size as they descended. Almost there.

Mitchell's cell phone dinged. He took it out and glanced at the text message that appeared.

You're still not listening, Mitch. Now the boy will pay.

Gunfire hit the helicopter's tail rotor.
The chopper lurched sideways and went into a spin.

Teddy screamed.

Mitchell white-knuckled the armrest, clamping his eyes shut.

Lord, keep us safe.

Would God hear his prayer after years of silence?

Hazel's stomach dropped as the helicopter spun. She heard Sami's desperate Mayday call in her headset, asking for emergency services to meet them. She informed them of the shots fired. Dispatch confirmed help was on the way. Hazel brought a screaming Teddy closer to her and nestled him under her arm like a mother eagle protecting her baby with powerful wings. *Lord, please help Sami gain control before we hit the ground.* Hazel willed her rapid heart rate to slow down. She had to stay strong for Teddy. "I've got you, bud. Stay close."

The boy inched closer, his little body quivering. "I'm. Scared," he said in between sobs.

Hazel had to keep him calm. *Pray in all situations. Remember, God is in the thunder.* Her mother's words.

She stole a glimpse at Mitchell and, from his strained expression, she guessed he also could use a good dose of divine intervention.

Hank sat stiff like a stuffed animal, biting his lip.

Even the burly man had fears.

Hazel closed her eyes. "Dear Jesus, be with us right now. Protect us and help Miss Sami to land this helicopter safely. Thank You. Amen."

Teddy stopped sobbing and tapped her arm with his free hand.

She opened her eyes. "What is it, sweetie?"

A huge tear welled before spilling onto his cheek. "You forgot to say 'in Jesus's name'. That's what my momma taught me."

She smiled. *Out of the mouth of babes.* "In Jesus's name, amen."

"Amen!" Teddy yelled.

At that moment, the helicopter righted itself and they hovered over the landing pad, swaying in the wind. *Come on, Sami. You've got this. Land us.*

As if hearing her silent encouragement, the chopper thudded to the ground.

The group lurched forward in their seats.

The helicopter stilled, and the whirling blades slowed.

Hazel let out an elongated breath.

"Jesus did it!" Teddy's enthusiastic words boomed in the aircraft.

"He sure did, bud." She tousled the boy's curls. "You were awesome." She glanced at Mitchell.

His entire body had tensed.

She let go of Teddy and leaned forward, placing her hand on his arm. "Mitch, you okay?"

"Did I ever tell you I don't enjoy flying?" He let out a shaky breath.

Why did he come with them, then? Was it for her? *No, don't go there. He wanted to save the boys.*

She patted his hand. "You did good too."

"Let's not do that again, okay?" Mitchell unbuckled his seatbelt.

"Anyone hurt?" Sami asked through the radio.

"We're all good," Hank replied.

Sirens wailed as firetrucks, police cruisers and an ambulance appeared on the scene, their lights flashing.

Constables hopped from their vehicles with their weapons raised. Hazel squeezed Teddy's free hand. "Help is here. It won't be long now and we'll have you back with your parents."

Hazel chewed the inside of her mouth, pushing back

the pending tears. Tears of relief but also anxiety. When would they find Jackson and Elijah? When would she have her son back safe in her arms?

God, make it so.

Her cell phone chimed, announcing a text.

She fished out her device and swiped the screen. Nora.

Hikers spotted the boys near Wild Rose Trail. I'm heading there now.

"What is it, Hazel?" Mitchell asked.

Obviously, her face revealed her alarm. She passed him her cell phone.

He read. "This is good news. We need to get there now."

"But that's close to the wildfire. Can you get an update?"

"I will as soon as we get out of here. Don't want to alarm anyone." His gaze shifted to Teddy.

"Understood. I'll check with Dad to see if he sent a search party there." She gazed out the window again. "Do you think the perpetrator is gone?"

"The what?" the boy asked.

Hazel chuckled. Leave it to a child to lessen the anxiety hovering within the helicopter. "The bad guy."

Teddy's face contorted. "Is he going to get me again?"

Mitchell squatted in front of the eight-year-old. "I won't let that happen. I promise." He released Teddy's seatbelt. "Time to go, bud."

Hazel's breath hitched at the tenderness in Mitchell's voice. Did he have a soft spot for children? His gentle expression told Hazel he did, and that opened her heart's wall a crack. Even though Garrison's abandonment still annoyed her after all these years, deep down, she longed for someone to share a life with her and Jackson. Someone to be a father to him.

Mitchell only wants to be friends, remember? And you don't need more heartache.

Hazel shifted her gaze back to the window. Constable Zeke Porter approached the chopper, and the paramedics were pushing a gurney across the airstrip. *Thank You, God. Right now, I need to get away from the man in front of me.* If only for a few moments.

The chopper door opened, and Zeke beckoned them out. "We need to get you out of here. Hazel, I'll take you and Mitchell back to your station."

"Thank you," Hazel said.

A masked Evan and Vanessa appeared in the doorway.

Teddy's widened eyes stared at the paramedics as he cowered further into his seat.

Hairs stood up on her neck. No, there's no way either of these paramedics would have pushed a child over the edge of a mountain. Would they?

Hazel shook off the crazy question and squatted in front of Teddy. "Sweetie, this is Evan and Vanessa. They won't hurt you. They're here to check you over and fix your arm."

"She's right, Teddy," Mitchell said. "They both just helped take care of my sister. You can trust them."

The boy nodded.

Mitchell helped Teddy exit the chopper. Hazel followed.

Evan smiled. "We're going to put you on this fun, rolling bed. Is that okay?"

Once again, Teddy nodded.

Hazel addressed Evan. "Be gentle with his arm."

The two paramedics carefully lifted the boy onto the gurney and began their examination of his injuries.

"I'm going to get an update on Bree and the fire. Meet

you in Zeke's cruiser." Mitchell jogged toward the hospital's entrance.

Two individuals ran toward them. Teddy's parents. Hazel needed to brief them before they reached the eight-year-old.

She approached them. "Mr. and Mrs. Hoffman, Teddy is okay. He may have a sprained arm, but the paramedics will get him into the hospital."

Mrs. Hoffman pulled Hazel into her arms. "Thank you for saving my boy. We've been worried sick."

Hazel understood.

The woman pushed back. "Is Jackson okay? The other boys?"

"We only found Teddy on the ledge. All the boys are accounted for, except Jackson and Elijah." Hazel failed to suppress the anxiousness in her voice.

"We're praying for a safe return," Mr. Hoffman said.

"Mama! Papa!" Teddy yelled.

Hazel turned at the boy's cry. "Go see your son. He's been very brave."

The couple beelined toward their child and hugged him.

A knot formed in Hazel's throat at the emotional reunion. Teddy clung to his mother while Evan and Vanessa tried to examine him. The boy wouldn't leave his mother's embrace.

Not that Hazel blamed him. It had been a rough two days for the little guy. Thankfully, she knew that both Elijah and Jackson were unharmed. But the question was, for how long?

She dug her fingernails into her palms, creating indentations. Hazel had to get to Nora's location and find them. She pivoted from the endearing reunion and sprinted toward the constable's cruiser.

An hour later, after gathering supplies and getting updates, Mitchell and Hazel approached Wild Rose Trail. Mitchell had checked in with Bree, and she'd reassured him she was fine. The doctors had treated her but wanted to keep her overnight for observation. Sergeant Stein had stationed a constable at her door. It was now late afternoon, and storm clouds had once again moved into the area. However, they could use the rain to help with the wildfires.

Lord, help us find those boys before the fire reaches us.

Mitchell's leader had reported that Kane was still MIA, and the team had called in another aerial drop. Hopefully, it would extinguish the fire.

Hazel stopped and put her hands on her hips. "Did you give your leader an update? I don't want you getting in trouble."

"I did. Surprisingly, Morgan was even nice to me." He chuckled. "Perhaps my charm is winning him over."

Somehow Hazel doubted that. The man had sounded harsh earlier. It was more likely that Supervisor Frank Hoyt had called him. Her father was good at manipulating people.

Did he want Mitchell around to protect Hazel?

Probably his only way of keeping tabs on his daughter, ensuring she wasn't alone.

"Hazel!" Nora appeared around a bend in the trail. "There you are. I didn't think you'd ever get here."

"We had to restock supplies and check in." Hazel grabbed her friend's arm. "Have you found anything?"

"Not yet."

Hazel looked around. "Where's the rest of the team?"

She pointed in the opposite direction. "Your father sent them that way."

"Why?" Mitchell asked.

"He felt it was the most likely spot Firebug would take the kids. But—"

"You disagree," Hazel said, finishing her friend's sentence. "Why?"

"Hikers reported suspicious activity on this side of the park. Plus I saw movement earlier—or at least I thought I did." She shifted her backpack. "Come on, we're wasting time." She hustled down the trail.

Hazel and Mitchell followed. The group searched for the next several hours, but came up empty. Had Nora been wrong and her father right? Hazel's shoulders slumped. They were losing daylight. Fast.

Hazel withdrew her radio. "I want to check in with Dad." She pushed the talk button. "Supervisor Hoyt, you there?"

She waited.

"Go ahead, Hazel. Any sightings?" her father asked.

"None. You?"

"Nothing. Duke hasn't picked up any further scents either. And Stein reported his forensics team didn't find any fingerprints on the teddy bear or bandana." He huffed. "Almost time to call it a night. I realize you don't want to leave the boys out there again, but you all need rest. You're not doing those kids any good if you're weak. You both have wounds to tend to. I'm heading back now. See you at the ranch." He clicked off.

Hazel sighed. Her father was correct, but her heart couldn't take another night of not having her son by her side.

Mitchell placed his hand on her back.

She startled at his approach. *Dad is right. My nerves are frayed and my body is weak.*

"Sorry, didn't mean to scare you." Mitchell drew out his water bottle and sipped. "He has a point."

She hung her head. "I know. It's just hard to leave my only child in the forest. Again."

Nora walked around the corner and caught up to them. "I heard what your dad said over the radio. Are we heading back? It's at least a good hour's hike to the station from here."

That would put them home after dark. "Yes, let's—"

A branch snapped to the right of them.

Hazel's hand flew to her gun.

"Don't even think about it," a menacing voice said.

They turned.

Two masked men approached with their weapons raised. "Stop right there. Throw your gun on the ground and kick it to me, Warden Hoyt."

She bristled. They knew her name. "Who are you?" She didn't recognize the raspy voice. She tossed her weapon.

The other person retrieved her gun and stuffed it into the back of his pants. "Not important. Now we need all your radios and cell phones. Hand them over."

Nora raised her hands. "Now, just wait a minute. What do you want from us?"

"It's not us you need to worry about."

Mitchell careened toward them.

The person to the right clocked him across the head before he could get any closer.

Mitchell slumped to the ground.

"Stop!" Hazel fell beside him. "Don't hurt him."

"Get him up," the other yelled.

She helped Mitchell to his feet. "You okay?"

He nodded, rubbing his forehead. "Gonna have a goose egg."

"That'll teach you to mess with us." He turned to his buddy. "Get their backpacks."

The man complied, wrenching them off each of them.

"Okay, get moving." The first suspect waved his gun toward the path to take them deeper into the woods. "Walk."

"Where are we going?" Nora's voice wavered.

"Not important. Just do what I say and you'll live." He paused. "Maybe."

The masked duo led them into a small opening, then pushed them forward. "Almost there."

Where were these men taking them?

The ground broke, and they plummeted into the earth. Hazel screamed as her arms flailed, trying to grasp anything, but it was no use.

One of the attacker's snickering registered in her brain along with his words. "Try to get out of this cage."

Nora screamed somewhere beside her.

Hazel hit the bottom, and pain pierced her side moments before her world turned black.

FIFTEEN

Pain jolted Mitchell awake and called out to him to run. To move. To do anything. Instead, he lay paralyzed, facedown, his breath shuddering in rapid bursts. The metallic taste of blood turned his stomach. *Move, Mitchell.* He moaned as a musty aroma bull-rushed him. Damp soil registered between his fingers and beneath him. Where was he? How long had he been unconscious? He willed himself to shake his foggy mind and opened his eyes. Darkness greeted him, and then he remembered.

The fall.

He gasped, rolled over and tried to sit.

Dizziness plagued him and he fell back down. A wave of nausea hit and he breathed in. Out. Pain throbbed in his side, where he'd been shot yesterday.

He peered upward from the pit, but only glimpsed a tree branch swaying in the wind against the gray sky. The fact that it wasn't pitch-black told him he'd only been out for a short period. Darkness hadn't totally descended.

"Hazel! Nora!" His cry squeaked out. He coughed to clear his dry throat. "Hazel! Nora!" Louder.

He slowly sat upright and fumbled for his flashlight, but remembered he'd put it in his backpack and the suspects had confiscated them. He shifted to his hands and knees, crawling as he felt around for the girls.

He bumped into something. "Hazel?"

She moaned.

Another groan sounded on the other side of him.

"Nora?" Thank God they were both alive. "Are either of you hurt?"

"I'm fine," Nora said. "I can't believe they led us into a trap." She laced her words with fury.

"Help me sit up," Hazel said. "Where did this pit come from, anyway?"

"They couldn't have built it in just an afternoon." Mitchell brought Hazel into a seated position. "Were you aware of this trap in your park?"

"Not at all. We would have filled it in. Too dangerous." She winced.

"What is it?"

"My side again."

A light glowed in the small area.

Nora raised a cell phone's flashlight.

"They didn't take your phone? Can you get a signal?"

"I had it in my side pocket. They missed it." She checked her screen. "No signal. We're too deep."

"Not surprised." Mitchell rubbed his forehead where the assailant had whacked him earlier. He'd need a pain medication soon or a migraine would manifest.

Nora shone her phone's beam around, revealing a small pit with roots growing out from the dirt walls.

Mitchell pushed himself upright as hope emerged. "We can get out using the roots." He turned to Hazel and helped her stand. "You okay to try?"

She bit her lip but nodded.

Mitchell pointed to Hazel's side. "Nora, shine the light there. I want to check her wound. Hazel, lift your vest."

"I'm fine." She squeezed her lips together.

"Don't argue."

Nora shone the light. "Hazel, listen to the man. I know you find it hard to take orders from others, especially men, but please do it so we can get out of here."

He didn't have time to figure out what her comment meant. Perhaps Nora had seen Hazel and her father arguing.

Hazel lifted her dirty uniform vest.

Mitchell examined her bandage. "Not good. You're bleeding again." He assessed the side of the pit. "I'm going to climb out. I need to get you to the hospital."

"Don't be silly," Hazel said. "I'll be fine. It's just a little blood."

"There you go, arguing again." Nora shone the beam upward. "He's right. We need to get out of here."

"Stand back." Mitchell pulled on a root, exposing it farther from the wall. He tugged on it and hoisted himself upward as he dug his feet into the dirt to brace his body weight.

Soil fell onto his face, and he froze. Memories flooded him, plunging him back to the grave where Ivy had buried him. Mitchell hesitated, frozen in time as he relived the terror. He had been immobilized because of the drug she'd given him. Shovelful after shovelful of dirt thudded on top of the crate she'd put him in, and some sprinkled through the cracks. The feeling of helplessness had washed over him and he had cried out to God to save him.

But God had let Ivy bury Mitchell that day and he'd almost died.

Perhaps God *had* saved him, but not until after Mitchell had passed out. Thankfully, his buddy Zac had tracked him down and saved him. That was when Mitchell's fear of tight spaces began.

God, why are You doing this to me again? Are You teaching me something?

A phrase his mother often said flashed through his mind.
In order to move forward in life, you need to look back at your troubles and deal with them. It's then you will find peace.

Was that true?

"Mitchell?" Hazel placed her hand on his back. "What's wrong?"

"I'm fine." He shook off the past, along with the dirt on his face, and plunged the toe of his boot into the wall, using the root as leverage.

He inched upward and reached the halfway mark. "Almost there," he yelled to the women.

He took another step and yanked on the root.

It came loose, and he fell backward. "Ugh!"

"Mitchell!" Hazel yelled.

He slammed into the dirt with a thud. Pain exploded and his heart pounded.

Hazel kneeled beside him. "Mitch, talk to me."

He wheezed and tried to sit.

She pushed him back down. "Stay still. Are you hurt?"

The pain subsided, and his pulse slowed. "Only my pride."

She swatted his chest. "Don't do that to me again. You scared the heebie-jeebies out of me!"

"The what?" He eased himself up.

"Never mind."

Nora shone the light again. "Well, perhaps I should try, since Hazel's side isn't good and I'm lighter than Mitchell."

Mitchell stood and dusted dirt from his cargo pants. "I'm afraid the roots aren't strong enough for you either. They're weaker at the top." *Kind of like your faith, Mitchell.* Where did the thought come from? Yes, his parents had raised both him and Bree in the church, so their deep-rooted faith was instilled in their children. He had let go of his as he grew older. It was weak both at the surface and deep down. Was God using this pit experience to show him it was time to get back to his roots?

Maybe.

"Mitchell, are you listening?"

Hazel's question thrust him back to their situation. "Sorry, what did you say?"

"What are we going to do?" Her voice quivered. "I need to get out of here and save my son."

The stress in her tone was clear. He squared his shoulders and once again inspected their pit with the help of Nora's light. "I will find a way. Nora, walk the wall with me so I can see what's beneath the soil better."

The duo circled around their dungeon pit and Mitchell inspected the wall, tugging on the roots. They all gave way. They would hold none of them.

Not good.

He turned to Hazel. "These aren't strong enough. I'm sorry."

She sank to the ground and buried her face in her hands. "God, why? Why?"

Seemed she also wrestled with God.

Mitchell sat in the dirt beside her and brought her into his arms. "I'm sorry I failed you."

She pushed back. "You didn't. You tried to save us."

He wiped a tear from her eye.

Nora cleared her throat.

Mitchell moved away from Hazel and stood. "Okay, we will get out of here. We just—"

A rustling noise came from above.

"Did you hear that?" he asked.

Movement sounded at the pit's opening.

"Help! We're down here," Mitchell yelled. He just prayed it wasn't the suspects returning to finish the job.

The women shouted.

A shadow passed above them.

"Nora, shine the light." Mitchell pointed. "Someone is up there."

She obeyed.

Two beady eyes glistened in the beam, staring back at them moments before it bared its teeth.

A cougar—not the rescue he'd hoped for.

Hazel's hand flew to her mouth to squelch the scream threatening to escape. *Wait, that's not right.* Staying silent and still wasn't the answer. She dropped her hand. "Guys, make lots of noise. Appear as big as you can. That will tell the cougar we're not easy prey. Flash your cell light around, Nora."

She raised the device, but seconds later, the light faded. "Great. Dead battery."

"Yell, everyone, and wave your arms." Hazel lifted her arms, flailing them while yelling as loud as she could.

The others did the same.

A light at the top of the pit flashed in the now-darkened night.

"Someone's up there." Hazel hopped up and down, ignoring the pain piercing her side. "We're down here! Help!" She just prayed the person holding the light was a friend and not foe.

The cougar shrieked its high-pitched scream before bounding away.

Hazel held her breath, waiting to see what other creature showed its face in the pit's opening.

A man peeked his head into the hole. "Howdy down there. Are y'all okay?"

Hazel turned to check on Mitchell.

His jaw hung open. Obviously, the man's sudden appearance had surprised him as well.

"Could this be our resident park vagrant the hikers have been talking about?" Nora's whispered question boomed in the small pit.

"Yes, ma'am. I am. Name's Vincent, but my friends call me Snake." He saluted the group. "Nice to meet you."

Snake? Odd choice for a nickname.

"Sir, can you help us get out of here?" Mitchell yelled.

The man disappeared for a second and returned, holding a bag. "Sure can. Got lots of items in my handy-dandy backpack. You'd be surprised at how many valuables I've collected. But first, call me Snake, not *sir*." He snorted while rustling through his bag, then held up a rope. "I'll tie this to a tree and throw the end to you."

Once again, he disappeared.

Nora pulled on Hazel's arm. "I'm not sure I trust a man who continually hides from us, living off the park's land. Do you think he'll hurt us?"

"I highly doubt it. He would've just walked by and left us here." Hazel glanced upward as the rope dropped into the pit.

Snake's face appeared. "Okay, who's first?"

The group looked at each other.

The man clucked his tongue. "Chop-chop. Don't have all day."

"Hazel." Mitchell grabbed the rope and held it out to her.

"No, send Nora." Hazel passed the cord to her friend. "Climb."

"Why me?" she asked.

"You're my friend and I want you to get to safety."

"But—"

Hazel jabbed her finger into Nora's shoulder. "Now look who's arguing. Time for you to go."

Twenty minutes later, the group was safely out of the hole. Hazel sat on the ground, breathing in the fresh air. "Thank you, Snake."

The gray-haired man with long, straggly hair raised his lantern and grinned. His smile displayed crooked teeth. "Anytime."

"Where did you get the name Snake?" Mitchell asked.

"My community gave it to me because I slither in and out of my hiding spots."

Nora brushed dirt from her uniform. "What are you hiding from?"

"People." He walked to a nearby tree and brought something out from behind the enormous trunk. "Found these. I assume they're yours," he said to Hazel and Nora, "since I see you're wearing park uniforms." He held up backpacks carrying Micmore National Park insignias.

"Yes." Hazel rose to her feet and took her backpack. She dug out water from her bag. "Where did you find them?"

Nora removed a radio from hers. "I'm going to report this incident." She walked away.

"Discarded at the end of Wild Rose Trail." He handed Mitchell the remaining bag. "I'm guessing whoever pushed you in that hole didn't think you'd live. Thankfully, Snake here came by and found you."

Hazel embraced the man. "Yes. Thank you for saving us. Why do you hide from everyone here in the park?"

"Because I know you won't let me stay if you find me. You see, my darling wife loved this park and I feel close to her when I'm here."

Sorrow filled Hazel over the love this man had for his late wife. His voice softened when he spoke of her. She released him and grazed his arm. "I'm sorry. How long ago did you lose her?"

"Ten years this fall. What's your name, Miss?"

"I'm park warden Hazel Hoyt." She held out her hand. "Nice to meet you, Snake."

"Oh, you're the rascal's daughter."

She chuckled. "Never thought of my father as a rascal, but yes, Supervisor Hoyt is my dad. Have you met him?"

Once again, the man clucked his tongue. "Heard him yelling at his employees the other day." He turned to Mitchell and shook his hand. "You are...?"

"Micmore Wildfire Unit's crew leader Mitchell Booth. I'd like to add my thanks to Hazel's for saving our lives and scaring the cougar away."

"Mighty happy to help. I hope you catch the stinker who's setting the fires."

"Snake, have you seen two young boys lost in the wilderness?" Hazel bit her lip. "We're desperate to find them."

"Oh. Wait here." He headed back down the trail and returned moments later with a boy by his side.

Hazel's heartbeat increased as they approached. Jackson?

The pair came into focus.

Not Jackson. "Elijah?" Hazel's legs buckled, worry over her still lost son consuming her body.

Mitchell grabbed her around the waist. "I've got you."

Hazel breathed in, willing strength into her legs, and broke free of his hold. "Snake, where did you find Elijah?" She kneeled in front of the boy. "Are you okay?"

He nodded.

"He was hiding in the bushes. Said he was running from a bad man. I checked him over. You see, I used to be a doctor years ago, before—" He paused. "Never mind. He's fine. No apparent physical injuries." Snake patted the boy's head. "When I heard you folks yelling, I told him to stay there while I checked out the ruckus. Thankfully, it was you and not the nasty people who've been chasing these young'uns. I found the boys at the loggers' cabin and fed them. I was going to get them back to the warden's station, but we got separated again."

Mitchell squatted in front of the boy. "How did you get away?"

"The man turned his back, and Jackson pushed him, then yelled at me to run. Told me to find you." His lower lip quivered. "You have to rescue him before the bad man hurts him."

Hazel's breath hitched. "How do you know he's going to hurt Jackson?"

"Because they said they hated you and you had to suffer for the sins you've committed."

Hazel staggered backward as questions bulldozed through her weary mind.

What sins? Why did these people hate her? What had she done to them?

A pinprick bit her neck, and she swatted at the attacking mosquito. Minutes later, her heart rate accelerated as nausea rose and the forest spun. She took a step, but lost her coordination and stumbled. Her vision blurred and realization dawned on her.

That wasn't a mosquito.

What exactly pricked her neck?

The question entered her mind moments before she fell into darkness.

SIXTEEN

"Hazel!" Mitchell pulled her into his arms, cradling her head. "Hazel, wake up!" What was wrong with her? He'd seen terror etch onto her face and transform her beautiful eyes into horror-struck ones seconds before she fell into a heap.

Elijah cried as Snake tried to console the boy.

Nora rushed around a cluster of trees. "What's going on? I just gave Supervisor Hoyt our location. He's on his way." She eyed Hazel. "What's wrong with my friend?"

Snake positioned himself next to Mitchell. "Let me look."

Nora wrenched the man backward. "This is all your fault. You did this!"

"I didn't, young lady. I used to be a doctor." He yanked his arm free and held out the lantern to Nora. "Hold this and simmer down."

She hesitated.

"Do it, Nora. Snake is only trying to help." Mitchell brushed hair off Hazel's face.

Nora held the light for Snake to examine his patient.

"What do you think happened?" Mitchell asked. "She has a knife wound on her right side. Could it have gotten infected?"

Snake gently lifted Hazel's shirt and peeled off a corner of the bandage. "Just dried blood. The dressing needs to be changed, though. Are you aware of any medical conditions?"

"No." He turned to Nora. "Are you?"

She shook her head. "None."

Snake patted the bandage back down before investigating her arms, then turned her head and peered closely at her neck.

And gasped.

"That's it." He pointed. "See that small reddened pinprick?"

"Yes. What is it?"

"I'd hazard a guess that it's some type of drug overdose." He stood. "Check for needles or anything on the ground. Whatever hit her in the neck is gone, and we need it to determine the drug."

"I saw her swat at something right before she fell." Mitchell felt around Hazel's body.

"What's that?" Nora asked, holding the light closer to a pile of rocks on the path.

A tiny dart lay next to a stone on the trail. It was so small and camouflaged that Mitchell had missed it.

Snake rummaged through his backpack and drew out a bag containing half a sandwich. He handed the food to Elijah. "You need this more than I do." He then scooped the dart up using the bag as a glove and turned it inside out to protect the dart from contamination. He handed it to Mitchell. "Get this to the authorities. You need to determine the drug type in order to treat her. Get her there now! I'm not sure how much time she has."

Mitchell's heart rate elevated at the man's authoritative command. He lifted Hazel into his arms, turning to Nora. "How far out is Frank?"

"Forty minutes."

"We don't have that long." How would Mitchell get Hazel to the hospital stat? *Think, Mitch.*

Sami. Her SAR helicopter was closer than the hospital's.

"Nora! Get Sami and her chopper here now. Tell them to meet us in the Wild Rose clearing north of where the trail intersects with Fireweed. It's not a large area, but we don't have any other choice." He turned to Snake. "You bring Elijah. We need you both to come too."

Mitchell didn't wait for a response, but raced toward the Fireweed/Wild Rose junction. *Lord, I'm sorry for walking away from You. Please don't take my disobedience out on Hazel.*

Come back to God.

His sister's words reentered his brain. Was it time to do that? His experience was too hard to mend. He had too much baggage. Would God still want him?

"Mitchell!" Nora caught up with him. "Sami is on her way and I've updated Supervisor Hoyt on the situation. He's contacting the hospital." She drew in a quick breath and continued, "He also reported that a constable will meet us at the hospital to get the dart, so a forensic toxicologist can determine the drug."

"Are they aware of the urgency?" Mitchell asked as they reached the clearing and stopped.

She nodded.

"I hope Sami gets here soon." Mitchell set Hazel delicately on the ground before bringing out his radio. "I need to apprise my leader of the situation. Stay with Hazel."

Nora nodded and sat down on the grass.

Mitchell pressed his radio button. "Morgan, you still on site?" He waited.

An owl hooted in the distance, reminding Mitchell of the late hour. He checked for wildlife in the area and prayed the cougar was long gone.

"Boomer, I'm here. What's your situation?"

"Transporting Hazel to the hospital. Possible drug overdose. I'll be off radar. Give me an update on the wildfires."

"Princess has relocated farther north and is giving me hourly reports. Doesn't look good there. Aerial support has failed to contain this one. Firebug seems to know the exact hotspots to cause the fires to spread quickly."

"Sounds like Firebug knows fires pretty well. Any idea of his identity?" Could it be one of their own? *Don't go there, Mitch.* "Perhaps someone who has a vendetta. Anyone like that cross your path in the years you've been fighting fires?" Mitchell turned his gaze back to Nora and Hazel. Snake had arrived with Elijah.

Now all we need is Sami. Hurry, Sami!

He kept his eye on Hazel and willed her to wake up. Mitchell's jaw tightened as the thought of losing this woman just after she reentered his life sent jolts of anxiety up his spine. Was his heart opening up again?

"The only arsonist in the Rocky Mountains area I remember is from years ago. A teenager started setting fires in abandoned warehouses, taunting us that we wouldn't be able to put the blazes out."

"Was he stopped?"

"Police never caught him, and the fires mysteriously ended. Thankfully, no firefighters were hurt. Only minor injuries." Rustling sounds sailed through the airwaves. "Wait, I think Smokey's father was on one of the last calls. I just wish we'd find Smokey."

Mitchell rubbed his brow. "I don't like it. I'm concerned something has happened to him."

"Me too. We're scouring the area. I'll keep you updated. You do the same."

"Will do." Mitchell shoved his radio into its holster

and jogged back to Hazel. "Has she moved or made any sounds?"

"Nothing." Snake placed his fingers on her neck. "Her pulse is still strong. That's good, but I don't like how her face has paled. She needs immediate attention."

As if in response, the familiar whomping sound of rotor blades invaded the night air. A spotlight appeared over the tree line, and as the chopper approached, wind assaulted them. Mitchell shielded Hazel from any potential flying debris as they waited for Sami to land nearby.

Thank You, Lord, for getting her here fast.

Sami jumped down from the helicopter and approached.

Another individual opened the side door and brought out a litter.

"That's Lenny. Our SAR medic," Sami said. "He'll examine her as we fly to the hospital. How's she doing?"

Lenny approached with the litter.

"Not good." Mitchell introduced Snake and gave the pair an update on Hazel's condition.

"Let's get her into the basket and into the chopper. Stat." Lenny squatted and quickly checked her vitals. "Pulse is steady at the moment. Let's go."

Six minutes later, doctors and crew met the chopper as they landed on the hospital's heliport. Lenny apprised them of Hazel's condition and they whisked her off into the building. Lenny escorted Elijah into the emergency area for examination. Nora had gone to the warden station and promised to contact his parents, asking them to come to the hospital.

Mitchell turned to Sami. "Thank you for getting her here so fast." He held out his hand.

Sami shook his hand. "My pleasure. I'm glad I could help. Hazel is known for her kindness and is well loved around these parts. I gotta get back. Will you be able to find other transportation back to the park?"

"Of course. I'll wait for a bit with Snake to get updates on Hazel. I also want to talk with Frank."

"Good. Godspeed." She hopped back into the chopper.

Mitchell and Snake walked through the emergency doors, directly into Supervisor Frank Hoyt's path. Hazel's mother, Erica, stood off to the side, biting her nails.

Frank shoved Mitchell. "How did you let this happen?"

Snake pressed forward. "It's not his fault, sir." He held up the bag. "This pierced Hazel's skin. You need to get it to toxicology right away."

Frank's eyes flashed. "And just who are you?"

"Sir, let me explain." Mitchell gestured toward Snake. "This is Vincent. He found Elijah and saved us all from the deep trap Firebug set for us. You should thank him."

Frank's gaze moved over Snake's appearance, then his eyes widened. "You're the vagrant living in our park."

Snake thrust his hand out. "Name's Snake. You're the rascal everyone talks about."

Frank ignored the man and hauled out his radio. "I'm getting the police to lock you up."

Erica placed her hand on her husband's arm. "Frank, leave it alone. He saved our girl's life."

Frank's expression softened, and he reholstered his radio. He snatched the bag from Snake. "I'll light a fire under the toxicology staff and get police protection for Hazel." Frank sprinted down the corridor as Sergeant Stein came around the corner. The two appeared to have a heated discussion before leaving the area.

"Mitchell, did Elijah say anything about Jackson's whereabouts?" Erica asked.

"He didn't know where he was, but he did say Jackson wasn't hurt." He hesitated. How much should he share with

Hazel's mother? "Mrs. Hoyt, somehow Firebug seems to know our every move."

She bit her lip. "I was afraid of that."

"What do you mean?"

Erica leaned closer and looked left, then right. "I believe someone employed by Frank is working with the Rocky Mountain Firebug."

A knot formed in Mitchell's stomach. "What? Why do you say that?"

"Because Frank's been getting threatening notes. Notes that have been left in places only his staff have access to."

Mitchell balled his hands into fists. Why was she just confessing this now? Could it be that Firebug's accomplice was right under all of their noses?

Who could they trust?

Hazel fought to open her eyes, but the heaviness kept them shut. Weariness plagued her, calling her back to sleep, but an irritating beeping prevented that from happening. Where was she? She moaned and turned her head.

"Hazel?" Mitchell's voice sounded nearby.

A hand grazed hers.

"Where am I? What happened?" Once again, she struggled to open her eyes. "Why am I so groggy?"

"You've been through a lot. What do you remember?" Mitchell asked.

Hazel searched the recesses of her mind, trying to piece the puzzle together. A dark pit, a screeching cougar, a man with long hair, and a little boy entered her brain.

Then the mosquito bite. Her hand flew to her neck. "I remember something biting me before my world turned black. Then strange dreams started."

"Can you open your eyes?" This came from another voice. One she didn't recognize.

"Who else is there and where am I?"

"You're safe and in your own room at the ranch," Mitchell said. "This is Dr. Jeremiah."

Finally, Hazel pried open her eyes, and her room slowly came into focus.

A tall, slender man dressed in a white lab coat with a stethoscope around his neck hovered over her. He took hold of her wrist. "How are you feeling?"

"Tired." She turned and spotted Mitchell sitting beside her bed. "What happened?"

His smile didn't match his twisted expression. "You were drugged by a dart. It wasn't a mosquito bite."

"Drugged?" She tried to sit, but the room spun.

"Take it easy." Dr. Jeremiah pushed her back onto the bed. "You need rest."

"Hazel, the dart contained large amounts of ketamine. It's amazing you survived." Mitchell paused. "You've been in and out of consciousness for two days. Your dreams were hallucinations. You woke several times, but you were incoherent."

She sprang upright in her bed, ignoring the white stars flashing in her vision. "Two days? Where is my son?"

"Elijah told us that Jackson was unharmed the last time he'd seen him. That's encouraging news." Mitchell also explained how Sami had airlifted her to the hospital. Her father had demanded a rush investigation on the drug, and once they'd determined the type, the doctors had treated her accordingly. She'd turned a corner but hovered in and out of consciousness. Her father had insisted they release her into Dr. Jeremiah's care so she could recuperate in her own bed. They finally relented and allowed her to leave. Her mother had talked her father into letting Snake stay at one of the Hoyt Hideaway cottages since he had saved her life with his quick diagnosis. Elijah had been checked and cleared. His parents were tearfully grateful to the group for his rescue. However, search parties had still failed to find Jackson.

"The wildfires have been contained. For now. Seems Firebug is taking a break. Why, we're not sure." Mitchell shifted in his chair as the door burst open.

Her parents entered.

"Honey, you're awake!" Her mother flew to her bedside. "We've been worried sick." She kissed Hazel's cheek and hugged her.

"How's she doing, Doc?" her dad asked.

"Her vitals are strong. Hazel, you may have lingering effects from the drug, but it's mostly gone. You're a fighter, that's for sure. I'll leave you guys alone now and I will be back later to check on you." Dr. Jeremiah packed his stethoscope into his medical bag. "Call me right away if her condition changes." He left the room.

Hazel turned to her dad. "What's happening with the search? Why haven't you found Jackson?"

"We've been doing everything we can, pumpkin. Firebug is hiding him well." He shoved his hands into his pockets. "I need to tell you something else."

"What is it, Dad?"

"I've been receiving threats."

"What? When?" Hazel coughed.

Her mother grabbed a water glass from the nightstand and helped her take a drink. "This isn't the time to discuss this. Hazel just woke up."

"Erica, she needs to be made aware."

Nausea attacked Hazel. "What? Tell me. Does this involve Jackson?"

Her father puffed out an elongated grunt. "A week ago, I received a threat that said I best pay up or my family will suffer the consequences."

Hazel fisted the comforter in her hands. "Pay up, why?"

"They said they needed money and knew I funded a local politician who apparently is dirty."

Hazel froze.

"When I found out, I cut him off and reported him." He walked to the window and pushed the drapes aside.

Dusk had fallen. Had she really slept for two days and now it was nightfall again? *Jackson, where are you? Lord, help him be safe.*

Her father let the drapes fall back into place. "I refused to pay and now Jackson is in danger. You were almost killed."

"Mom, did you know this?"

Her gaze dropped to the floor. "I only found out a few days ago. He wouldn't let me tell you."

Heat flushed Hazel's body. "How could you?"

"I was only trying to protect this family," her father said.

Mitchell stood. "I should leave you guys alone."

Hazel grabbed his hand. "No. Stay." He was the only person who hadn't betrayed her.

She glanced at her mother and father. "Get out, both of you."

Her father hesitated. "Pumpkin, I'm sorry."

"Stop calling me that. I don't want you here. You've done a lot of damage over the years, Dad, but this takes the cake. Get out!" Wheezing breaths consumed her. She inhaled deeply to steady her breathing, hoping to curb the anger raging inside.

Her parents left and closed the door.

Mitchell held the straw to her mouth. "Drink. Just so you know, your mother told me they suspect someone close to the family is behind the threats. She told me about them when you were at the hospital. I'm so sorry."

Hazel held the straw and sipped the water. "How's Bree doing?" She had to take her mind off her parents.

"Much better, but still recuperating. We actually relocated her here for protection."

Hazel lifted herself up on her elbows. "Where is she? I want to see her."

Mitchell set the glass on the stand and eased Hazel back down. His fingers caressed her arm. "In the cabin next to mine. You need to get better first. I thought I lost you. You scared me."

Hazel ignored what his touch did to her and contemplated his words. What did he mean? Her eyes locked with his.

He caressed her face with the back of his hand. "Hazel, I can't pretend any longer. You almost died, and it made me realize something."

Did she want to listen to his confession? She held her breath and gazed into his gorgeous green eyes. "What?"

"I don't think of you as a little sister. I know you heard me say that to Bree, but I was wrong." His eyes fell to her mouth. "Actually, I've realized I never did."

Her breath hitched. "What are you saying?"

He stood and paced the room. "I need to tell you about Ivy."

Here we go. He's in love with someone named Ivy. She swallowed the thickening in her throat. She didn't have the strength to deal with rejection right now.

"I met her at church after I moved to Ontario. Her long red curls and bright blue eyes immediately caught my eye. We first went out for coffee, and it blossomed from there. I fell hard—fast." He stepped to the window. "But then—" He stopped.

"What?"

He turned, and his eyes flashed hatred.

If that was possible for such a gentle man.

He returned his gaze to something outside her window. "She became obsessive."

"What do you mean?"

"Simple things at first. She'd ask what I was doing on the nights we didn't have dates planned."

"What's abnormal about that?"

"Nothing, but it became a constant question. Then she started following me when I left my condo. I asked her why and she made up an excuse she was only in the area." Another hesitation. "I bought it at first, because I was in love—or thought I was. So, I ignored the signs. Bree came to visit me and I introduced them. My sister saw right through Ivy and tried to warn me. Bree and I had a huge fight, and she left on the next plane. Something I've regretted for two years."

That was why Bree had stopped talking about him. It was too painful. "What happened then?"

"Ivy would call or text me like ten or more times a day. Then friends started warning me she'd been calling them, checking up on me. I finally broke it off." Once again, he turned to her. "After that, her obsession escalated."

She shifted in her bed, trying to get comfortable. "How?"

"She began stalking me. I'd see her everywhere when I was out. Plus she watched my condo. One time in the middle of the night, I got up to get some water and looked out the window. She stood next to her car, watching me. Another night, she tried to break in. I called the cops and reported her." He rubbed the back of his neck. "I even took out a restraining order, but in the end, that still didn't help."

"What happened?"

"I was going to meet my friend Zac for a hockey game. I had just finished a tough shift of fighting a fire an arsonist had set. I needed to grab my clothes from my truck and

I wasn't paying attention. I dropped my keys and then felt a pinprick. I guess, similar to what you felt. Anyway…she gave me a drug that immobilized me but kept me alert."

How could anyone be so cruel? Hazel bit her lip as she waited for Mitchell to continue.

"She took me to a cemetery where she'd dug a grave."

"What?"

"Yup. Told me if she couldn't have me, no one could. Because of my rejection, I had to die."

Tears formed in Hazel's eyes. Thankful tears that he'd survived, but also tears of sympathy for the terror he'd encountered. "I'm so sorry you went through that. How did you escape?"

"My buddy Zac Turner was aware of my restraining order against Ivy—he's a police officer—and when I didn't show up for the afternoon hockey game, he got worried." He smirked. "I guess you could say my obsession with hockey saved my life." Then his expression sobered. "Ivy made one mistake. She forgot to check me for my phone. I had stuffed it in the inside of my jacket. Zac determined my last known location at the gravesite, before she buried me. His detector dog, Ziva, found me. Because I hadn't showered before she kidnapped me, they gave Ziva the accelerant scent used in the fire and she led them right to the grave Ivy had buried me in. Thankfully, they caught her and charged her with attempted murder."

"That's why you reacted in the pit when the dirt fell on you."

"Yes. I almost died in that grave. Zac saved me." He bit his lip.

Hazel held out an outstretched hand. "Come here."

He sat on the bed and intertwined his fingers with hers. "God looked after me that day, so why can't I seem to deal with the past and give Him my trust?"

Something she too struggled with doing. "I wish I had the answer to that question."

He rubbed his thumb along the back of her hand. "Hazel, I'd like to be part—"

She yanked her hand away, interrupting his words. She refused to hear what Mitchell was about to say, because of Garrison's betrayal. It had been years, but it felt like yesterday. As strong as her feelings were for Mitchell, she couldn't open her heart. Her fears held her back.

Let it go, Hazel.

Like Mitchell, why couldn't she deal with the baggage Garrison had left behind? Plus her father's latest betrayal only added to it.

She eyed the man before her and noted the confused look on his handsome face. He'd put his heart out there and she'd smashed it.

But she couldn't give him her whole heart when pieces of it lay shattered in the past. And—

She needed to find her son.

Mitchell's cell phone rang. He stood and fished it out of his pocket. "Booth here." His eyes widened. "What? Where?" A pause. "Okay, I'll be there as soon as I can." He clicked off.

"What is it?"

"Firebug started another fire, and it's close. I need to stop it now. Please rest. Let your father find Jackson." He left the room.

Like that was gonna happen.

She flung off the comforter and swung her legs over the bed, sitting on the edge. The room spun, but she ignored it and stood. She teetered and grabbed the nightstand.

And fell to the floor, bringing the lamp crashing down with her.

Her mother appeared in the entranceway and helped

Hazel back onto the mattress. "Sweetie, you're in no condition to be getting out of bed."

Hazel sobbed. She no longer held in the tears.

Her mother embraced her, rocking her like she was still five years old. "Honey, let your father find Jackson. You need sleep."

Hazel bit back angry words. Her mother was right. She was too weak. She nodded and let her mother tuck her back under her comforter.

Tomorrow. She'd find Jackson after a good night's sleep.

Her door swung open, bringing in the morning light and jolting her from restless nightmares of Jackson being stalked by a cougar.

The light flicked on. "Hazel! Your father's been kidnapped."

She bolted upright in bed. "What?" *Lord, what are You doing?*

Had the person threatening her father made good on his word and gotten to Frank Hoyt?

Remorse hit Hazel hard. Remorse over the last angry words she'd spoken to her father. Remorse for years of holding her bitterness inside and not dealing with it properly. If she had, would she have been so harsh with him?

Would Hazel ever be able to say she was sorry?

She had to try.

Her cell phone vibrated on her nightstand. She picked it up and read the text.

You're a cat with nine lives. Well, now we have your son and father. You took something from me and now we've taken something from you. Let's play a game of hide 'n seek, shall we? Come and find us. If you can. Do NOT tell the cops or your son will pay. Firebug

Hazel pulled her shoulders back. Time to come up with a plan to end this sick game.

Once and for all.

SEVENTEEN

Mitchell wiped his forehead with the back of his hand and exited their makeshift EOC. He'd stayed close to the team overnight to help fight the blaze ravaging the area close to Hazel's park station and her home. He peered through his binoculars and surveyed the wreckage from Firebug's latest wildfire. Acres destroyed, but his team's control line had held and successfully contained the spread. They now kept watch for smoldering embers.

Mitchell ducked and walked back inside the tent to grab a quick breakfast. He had to check on Hazel's condition. He replayed their conversation from last night over and over. It screeched in his head like an old VHS tape on rewind. He'd totally opened up, but she'd rejected him. Had he been so wrong and misjudged the signs? The looks they'd shared?

No, he was sure he'd seen something in her wide hazel eyes. Something that held her back. But what?

Mitchell gritted his teeth and picked up his coffee mug. He required caffeine to jolt him awake.

"What's going through that head of yours?"

Mitchell flinched and turned, spilling his coffee on his shirt. He brushed the liquid off.

He hadn't heard his leader enter the unit's tent.

"Just trying to wake myself up from a tough night." He raised his cup. "You make excellent coffee."

He had to steer the conversation to his team and not his thoughts.

Morgan walked to the long food table and poured himself a cup, snatching a donut. "Good job in directing the team last night. I was wrong about you."

Mitchell suppressed his shock at his leader's words. "What do you mean?"

"I hated the fact Randy pushed you on me, requesting you to be the unit leader. I wanted it to be Smokey, but now I realize Smokey isn't ready." He bit into his treat and chewed before continuing. "You're good at what you do and effective at leading others."

Wow. He didn't think his day would start with compliments from his crusty leader. Maybe Mitchell had judged Morgan incorrectly. "Thank you, sir. I appreciate you saying so." He sipped his coffee. "Anything on Smokey?"

"None. It's almost like he's hiding from us."

"Or Firebug. Perhaps Smokey knows who he is and doesn't want to be found."

"Are you a praying man, Boomer?"

"That's a loaded question. I was at one point, but I'm afraid I've fallen away from God." Mitchell gazed out the tent's opening. "You?"

"Yes, and I admit I can be grouchy at times. I'm sorry for being so hard on you, son." He walked over and placed his hand on Mitchell's shoulder. "Come back to God. He's waiting."

Mitchell turned. "You sound like my sister."

"She's a smart woman." He finished his coffee and threw the cup in the trash. "I'm going to go check—"

Mitchell's cell phone buzzed. He removed it from his side pocket and checked the screen. Hazel.

Dad's been kidnapped. I need you.

Mitchell sucked in a breath.

"What is it?" Morgan asked.

"Frank Hoyt's been kidnapped. I need to get back to the ranch. Hazel asked for my help. Is that okay?"

"Go. I've got things here and I'll keep you updated."

Ten minutes later, Mitchell bounded up the Hoyt Hideaway Ranch's front steps, but before he could knock, Hazel opened the door.

"I'm so glad you're here." She fell into his arms and sobbed. "What more can Firebug take from me?"

Mitchell held her tight. "I'm so sorry. What are the police doing about it?"

She stepped back and lifted her cell phone. "They warned me not to tell them."

Mitchell read the text. "We need to do something. What do they mean by a game of hide-and-seek?"

"I played it all the time with Jackson." Her eyes widened. "Mitch, this is someone who knows me personally, but who?"

"We can't trust anyone." He studied her ashen face. The dark circles under her eyes betrayed her physical state. "How are you feeling?"

"Fine."

"Liar. I can see it on your face." He guided her to the door. "Let's get you inside and come up with a plan."

She allowed him to escort her into the foyer of their family home.

"My dad's ranch foreman, Rusty, is in the kitchen with Mom and Bree." Hazel seized his hand and led him down the corridor and into the large kitchen and dining area. "Mom, Bree, Mitch is here to help."

His sister rushed to his side and hugged him.

"Bree, what are you doing out of bed?" he asked.

She stepped away and swatted his arm. "I'm fine. Hazel's mom had Dr. Jeremiah check on me at the cabin earlier this morning. He said I'm getting stronger. I want to help too."

His gaze shifted from his sister to Hazel. "No, you both have been through too much." He addressed Rusty. "Are you aware of the situation?"

"Yes. Erica brought me into the loop." The older man squeezed Erica's arm. "We'll find Frank."

"I've also sent for Snake," Hazel said. "He's on his way here."

Mitchell leaned closer to her. "Can I talk to you privately?"

She nodded and staggered into the hallway. "What is it?"

"Do you think it's wise to trust both Snake and Rusty?"

"Well, they're not the police, and Dad trusts Rusty with his life. He's been his foreman since I was a little girl." She bit her lip. "And Snake saved our lives. He also knows how to hide in our park, so he may be aware of some places we don't."

He couldn't argue with her reasoning. It made sense. "Okay, but you let us do the searching and involve no one else."

"Got it."

A knock sounded at the front door.

"That's Snake. I'll let him in and we'll make a plan." Hazel sauntered down the hallway.

Mitchell inspected her closely, noting her weakened state.

No way would he let her out in her condition.

I will find your father and son, Hazel. Even if it costs me my life.

* * *

Hazel checked her watch for the fifth time, chewing on her bottom lip. Was it only an hour ago that the men left to search for her father and son? Her mother sat across from her in the living room while Bree rested in the guest room down the hall. Seemed like she'd lied to her brother when she said she felt better. Hazel had to admit too that her energy had waned, and she was thankful for the small group of men who were out searching. They'd let no one else know. They weren't sure who to trust.

Once again, the last statement she'd spoken to her father tumbled through her mind.

I don't want you here.

Would they be the final words she'd ever say to him? *No, Lord. I need to fix this.*

She failed to contain her tears, and they flowed freely down her face.

Her mom moved to the couch beside her, bringing Hazel into her arms. "We'll find them, sweetie."

"My last words to dad—and you—were cruel. I'm sorry, Mom. I didn't mean them." She nestled into her mother's embrace and sobbed.

"Shh… Sweetie, it's okay. You're under pressure and worried sick about Jackson." She smoothed Hazel's disheveled hair. "God's got this."

Hazel popped her head up. "How can you stay so calm?"

"Inside, I'm terrified, but I've learned throughout the storms in life that God doesn't give us more than we can handle. He's right there with us in the thunder. We just need to look to the horizon."

"Mom, why is Dad so harsh to everyone?" Hazel asked. "Jayla has come to grips with his abrasive demeanor, but I can't."

"That's because they had a heart-to-heart talk and got their feelings all out on the table. You need to do the same."

"Why can't he tell me he's proud of me, though? He picks apart everything I do."

Her mother shook her head. "You're wrong. He's proud of all his kids, but has a hard time showing it. You wanna know why?"

"Yes."

"Deep down, he feels like he's a failure."

Hazel's jaw dropped. "What? He excels at everything he does."

"Because he couldn't stop Kyle from taking his own life. His death ripped your father inside and out. Ever since then, he's not only tough on himself but all of you. It's only because he loves you and is so scared of losing his children, like he lost Kyle."

Hazel winced. Losing her younger brother to suicide was the toughest thing her family had faced. She didn't realize her father blamed himself. But then again, she was now a parent and understood his thinking. Failing to find her son gnawed at her every hour as the what-ifs plagued her mind.

She flew off the couch. "I have to tell Dad I'm sorry and I understand. I keep wondering what I could have done better to protect Jackson."

Her mother stood. "Hazel, you are an amazing mother. Don't think that way."

She hugged the woman. "Thanks, Mom, for telling me about Dad."

"They'll find him. And Jackson. Just you wait and see."

Several hours later, in the early evening, the men stomped their feet as they entered the foyer.

Hazel greeted them. "Anything?"

Mitchell frowned and shook his head. "I'm sorry. We've searched every place we could think of."

"He's right," Snake said. "I also took them to all of my hiding spots. It's like they've vanished."

Hazel collapsed to the floor. "No! You need to find them."

Mitchell squatted and took her hands in his. "It's not safe out there now. Storms are hammering the region again. I'm sorry."

"We're going to determine our plan for tomorrow," Rusty said. "Erica, are you okay if we discuss this in your kitchen?"

"Of course. I'll put the coffeepot on. I think it's gonna be a long night."

Hazel pushed herself up. "I need to be alone. God and I have to talk." She hurried to her room, plunking herself on the bed. A plaque on her wall caught her attention. The scene revealed a crooked path through a densely wooded area. The verse above it read:

A man's heart deviseth his way: but the Lord directeth his steps. Proverbs 16:9.

Her mother had bought it for her after Jackson was born, to remind her of God's guidance in their paths in life. Hazel's perfectionist personality liked to sketch out every detail in her daily, monthly and yearly schedule. And when that failed, she too, felt like she'd failed.

Her mother knew her daughter well. *Thanks, Mom, for jogging my memory.* God was in control of the details. Not Hazel.

"God, I continue to disappoint You, don't I?" Tears rolled down her cheeks as she rewound events in her life. Events she must deal with and move on from, especially when it came to her father. *Forgive.* The word seemed simple, but it was the hardest thing in life for her. That and surrendering all details of her life to God.

It was time.

Hazel slipped to the floor and kneeled facing her bed, clasping her hands together. Her favorite position for getting serious with God. "Lord, forgive me for not trusting You. For not giving You every aspect of my life. I'm sorry. Thank You for showing me I need to forgive Dad. Please give me the chance to tell him. Save him and Jackson. Bring them home to us." She inhaled and wiped away an escaped tear.

"I surrender my life back to you. Take it and do with it what You will. Even if what comes my way isn't what I had planned or expected. Help me to trust." Her voice quivered.

"No matter what. In Jesus's name, amen." She crawled back into bed as a word etched into her mind, giving her peace.

Freedom.

Freedom from the past. Freedom from the anxiety of what lay ahead. Freedom from her failures.

Hazel's cell phone buzzed, jarring her awake. She sat up and checked the clock on her nightstand. Two o'clock. Had Mitchell and the others left? Lightning flashed, illuminating her room. She stilled, her fears of storms returning. *Freedom.* Could she give that anxiety over to God too?

She picked up her phone and swiped the screen.

A video and message appeared in her text.

Your team is poor at seeking. Come to the old lookout at park station #7 if you want to see your son and father alive. And Hazel, tell no one, or they die. Firebug

She held her breath and pressed Play.

Her father and Jackson appeared on the screen. They squirmed as they sat side by side with gags covering their mouths. "Olly olly oxen free," a distorted, menacing voice said. "Time to surrender and sacrifice yourself for these two."

Her father's eyes widened, and he shook his head frantically, mumbling.

The camera operator laughed. "Aw… Daddy doesn't want you to, but Hazel, we're not kidding around. Come alone. If you tell anyone, they die. We will know."

The screen went dark.

Lord, what do I do?

Thunder rumbled and shook the house.

God is in the thunder too. Her mother's words returned, bringing Hazel peace.

An image of her son's bread crumbs flashed in her mind, instantly giving her a plan.

Thank You, Lord.

She prayed for strength before climbing out of bed and getting dressed. Then she scribbled a message on a small piece of paper and raced out the ranch's front door, watching for any movement on the property. She skulked from tree to tree and made her way to Mitchell's cabin. Looking in both directions, she slid the note under the door before heading to her vehicle.

Five minutes later, she ran up the steps of her park station and unlocked the entrance, running to the supply room. She gathered her weapon, along with a knife she concealed in an ankle holster. On the way out of the room, she snatched two radios before heading to the stable. She entered Chestnut's stall and prepared her horse for the trek to Micmore Ridge. The lookout at Park Station #7 wasn't accessible by motorized vehicles. The pelting rain would make it hard for her and Chestnut, but she trusted his steady footing. Hazel holstered one radio on her hip and stuffed the other into the saddle's pouch. Before leading her horse from his stall, she placed a handful of buttercup flowers along with her warden hat on the hook by Thunder, praying Mitchell would understand.

She clucked her tongue. "Let's ride, Chestnut. I'm counting on you." She mounted him and squeezed her legs, veering him out of the stable and onto Buttercup Trail.

Time to face the Rocky Mountain Firebug head on.

Even if it meant sacrificing herself.

Thunder shook the small cabin, jolting Mitchell awake. He shot into a seated position and placed his hand on his chest to calm his racing heart. Storms normally didn't bother him, but something unsettled him in the early morning hours. Lightning flashed, spotlighting a small piece of paper by the door. Mitchell got out of bed and snatched it up, turning on the light to read.

Take Thunder and look for the crumbs along the trail. Hurry. Tell no one. H.

Hazel's cryptic note sent trepidation coursing through Mitchell's veins. What was Hazel trying to tell him? He tapped his chin. Then it dawned on him. Hazel referred to Jackson's bread crumbs. She spoke about them on their horseback ride a few days ago.

Hazel needed his help. Determination squared his shoulders. He hastily dressed in a blue plaid shirt and cargo pants before grabbing his cell phone, radio, flashlight and a pocketknife—the only weapon he had—before barreling out the door.

Five minutes later, he parked in front of the stable at Micmore National Park and sprinted inside, looking around.

Where was the bread crumb? *Come on. Show me, Hazel.*

Thunder whinnied, drawing Mitchell's attention to his stall door.

And Hazel's cowboy-like warden hat hanging on a nail with buttercup flowers tucked into the rim.

Her bread crumb telling him to follow the Buttercup Trail. A question lingered as he quickly saddled Thunder.

How much time had passed since she left the note and clues?

God, help me find her before it's too late.

EIGHTEEN

Rain pelted, soaking Hazel to the core. She adjusted the light she'd fastened on a helmet before leaving the stable. The beam helped her navigate in the early morning hours. A flash of lightning brightened the trail as visions of the night her fear of storms began. She'd had a fight with her father over why he wouldn't let her drive her friends to the after-prom party. She stormed out, grabbing his keys. Her rebel nature cost her dearly that day. She'd been taking the curve too fast in a storm and hydroplaned, crashing into a tree. One of her high school friends had been in the passenger seat and almost died. All because of Hazel's stubborn nature. She never should have been driving. Her inexperience nearly cost a friend their life and instilled a fear of thunderstorms. Ever since that night, her strained relationship with her father had escalated.

Thunder clapped, jolting both her and Chestnut. *Pay attention, Hazel. Don't make the same mistake.* Jackson and her father required her help.

Hazel stopped at a fork in the trail and dismounted. She stuck another buttercup flower in between a rock formation. She prayed Mitchell understood her note. Hazel had to be cryptic, just in case Firebug's spies found it. She couldn't let them know she'd asked for help.

She mounted Chestnut and nudged him toward Micmore Ridge. Daylight had crested, but the stormy clouds had kept the wilderness a murky gray. The trail led upward and Chestnut's hooves slipped on wet stones. Hazel held the reins tighter. *Steady, boy. You've got this. We're almost there.* Hazel refused to go faster. She wouldn't make that mistake again. A saying entered her mind. *Slow and steady wins the race.*

But would their slow approach cost her father and Jackson their lives?

Thirty minutes later, after a difficult trek, Hazel tethered Chestnut under an abandoned, sheltered lean-to connected to a small shed at the base of the old station. She'd proceed on foot up the steep trail to the lookout. A question formed in her mind. Hadn't the search parties checked this area? They'd probably missed it because they were aware of the dangerous rocky terrain and rickety structures.

Hazel's breath labored as she hiked the steep slope to the lookout. She noted the darkened, tiny building. No signs of life were evident. However, that meant nothing. She had to investigate, but she required stealth mode and turned off her light. She prayed for safety and placed one foot on the weathered step to test its sturdiness. It held, and she gingerly advanced upward, holding the wobbly railing. Reaching the top, she wiped the dust from the small window and peered inside. A flash of lightning revealed her father and son sitting in wooden chairs, tied and gagged. She clasped her hand over her mouth to squelch her cries of relief. Her son and father were alive. *Thank You, Lord that they're safe.* For now. She moved to the next window and repeated the same process so that she could observe the rest of the room.

Empty.

Odd. Why would Firebug leave them alone?

She shivered as a foreboding shudder crept through her

body. Something wasn't right, but she couldn't wait. *Lord, help me get in and out with no one seeing me. I have to save them.*

Hazel tried the doorknob. Unlocked.

Another wave of worry attacked her body, but she ignored it and unleashed her weapon and opened the door.

She entered, waving the gun in all directions before turning her gaze to her father.

His widened eyes glistened as tears formed. He shook his head as if telling her to go away. *Not happening.*

She rushed to his side and took off his gag. "Daddy, you okay?"

"She's close, pumpkin. Take Jackson and run!" Her father's raspy words revealed his anxiousness.

"Nope. We're all getting out of here together." Her fingers shook as she removed Jackson's gag. "Baby, I'm so glad to see you. Are you okay?" She couldn't hide the quiver in her voice. A teardrop tumbled down her cheek.

"Yes, Mama," he said. "Don't cry. You found me. You followed my bread crumbs."

She untied his hands and brought him into her arms. "I did, baby. You're so smart."

"Mama, I asked you not to call me that. I'm not a baby."

Hazel hugged him tighter and chuckled. "I'm sorry, Jackson. I just missed you so much."

"We gotta run now. The bad lady will be back."

Hazel broke free of their hug and untied her father. "Dad, who is it? It's someone close to us."

"Not sure. They wore masks and only spoke in raspy whispers." He stood and hugged her. "Hazel, I'm so sorry I've been hard on you."

She released him. "No, Dad. It's me who needs to apologize. I haven't been a good daughter, and for that, I'm sorry. I shouldn't have blamed you and told you to get out of my room. You did what you did to protect your family."

He shook his head. "No, I've failed my family too much. Can you ever forgive me for all my stupidity and times I was tough on you? You're an excellent park warden and an even better mother." He caressed her cheek. "I'm so proud of you. I don't tell you enough, and that ends today. From now on, I'll be your first champion in everything you do."

"Of course, I forgive you—if you can forgive me."

The normally stoic man's lip quivered. "I've been a foolish old man ever since Kyle died."

"Dad, Kyle's death was not your fault. You can't blame yourself."

"A parent should know when their child is hurting, especially enough to commit suicide. I missed the signs, Hazel. After that day, I told myself I'd watch you all carefully and never let it happen again. The problem was, I held on too tightly. Now all my kids hate me."

"That's not true, Dad. We just didn't understand."

"I'm sorry."

Hazel hugged him. "I love you, Daddy."

"Love you too, pumpkin."

Clapping sounded behind them. "Aw…so touching. Drop your weapon and turn around slowly. Now!"

Hazel bristled. She recognized that voice. She pivoted and came face-to-face with Firebug's accomplice.

"Nora?"

The woman had a Glock pointed directly at Jackson.

Hazel noted the flash of detest on her coworker's face. Gone was the kind-hearted Nora Martin that Hazel once knew. Or—at least—thought she knew. What possessed the woman to stoop to criminal activities? "Why, Nora? Why? I thought we were friends." Betrayal hit Hazel, hard—

ening her stomach. How could she have been such a bad judge of character?

Nora stepped toward Jackson and lifted her gun higher. "I said put your weapon down. Now!"

Hazel held both hands in the air. "Okay. Okay. Please don't hurt us." She bent down, keeping her eyes on Nora, and set her firearm on the floor before returning to an upright position.

"Kick it to me."

Hazel obeyed.

Nora walked over to Hazel. "Good girl." She took her cell phone and radio from her holster. She patted her waistline and back. "Now we wait."

"Wait for what?" Hazel's Dad asked.

"Mitchell, of course." Nora sneered at Hazel. "We know you tipped him off. My love will greet him soon with a wonderful surprise. Then you all die."

No! Mitchell was walking into a trap. *Lord, show me what to do. You know I love him. I want to tell him.*

Stall. The word came to her with a flash of lightning moments before the thunder boomed.

She had to keep talking to give herself time to come up with a plan. "Nora, tell me why you're doing this. Why kidnap my son?"

She stood eye to eye with Hazel. "Because I hate you. Hate all Hoyts."

The anger radiating off Nora caused Hazel to stumble backward. "What did we do to you?"

Nora waggled her index finger in Hazel's face. "You stole my job!" She redirected her attention to Frank Hoyt. "And you have not only been cruel to everyone, but you know I deserved the warden's position. I was next in line for a promotion. But no, you had to give it to your incompetent daughter."

Hazel's dad stepped forward, eyes flashing. "How dare you. Hazel deserved the position. You were not ready."

She waved the gun in his face. "Step back, Supervisor Hoyt, or I will shoot your daughter right now."

He complied.

"I deserved it. I'd been working two years before Hazel joined the Micmore National Park staff. Two. Years." She mumbled under her breath and glanced back at Hazel. "You only got the job because you're the supervisor's daughter."

How could anyone have so much hatred and jealousy flowing through them to even think of taking lives? This Nora Martin was definitely not the one Hazel recognized. Wait. She was doing this for Firebug. "Tell me. How long have you loved the Rocky Mountain Firebug? Did he coerce you into his nasty game?"

"He didn't have to. I volunteered to be part of his retribution on firefighters." She smirked. "And yes, I love him. We're getting married soon."

"Who is he and why does he hate firefighters?" Hazel asked.

"You'll find out soon enough." She pushed another chair close to the two sitting in the middle of the room. "Everyone sit. Time to get ready for the big event."

"Tell me how you've been helping Firebug." Hazel ignored Nora's command to sit.

Nora raised her gun again. "Simple. I texted you, pretending to be Firebug. Spied on you. Planted trackers everywhere. In the horses' saddles, in your gear. I also planted listening devices in the park station. My love placed them in Mitchell's radio too. Plus hidden cameras on the Hoyt Hideaway Ranch. We knew where you were at all times. We found some of Jackson's bread crumbs and used them to scare you. It worked too."

Hazel's father lunged toward Nora, nostrils flaring. "How did you get onto my property?"

Nora raised the gun higher. "How do you think? We bought off one of your ranch hands."

"Who?" he asked.

"Johnny boy. Seems he needed money to put his baby brother through college. Step back."

He did as she said.

Hazel guessed her father's thoughts. He had needed an extra ranch hand in a hurry and hired John a few months ago. However, he'd obviously failed at vetting John closely and had paid the price. Hazel turned to Nora. "But who attacked us at Wild Rose Trail and pushed us into the pit?"

"That was the brilliant part of my love's plan. He sent two hired thugs to push us in. I just had to lead you there. Make it look good. Firebug was going to kill both you and Mitchell. Then save me. However, Elijah and Snake ruined the plan when they showed up."

Fire exploded throughout Hazel's body, and she clenched her fists. "Did you have Jackson and the boys kidnapped? Why?"

"Yes. I arranged for those men to get to the scout camp while my love set the fire. That was an act. He didn't push me hard. I just pretended to be unconscious. I let the paramedics take me and then woke up at the hospital. Fooled you all. I also planted a pig-blood arrow on the rocks so you'd take that path. Too bad you survived the ketamine overdose." She pointed the gun at Jackson. "Doesn't matter. Your nine lives end here. Tie up your son and father. Now!"

Lord, I don't see a way out of this. Please. Show me.

Her father and Jackson sat in the chairs and Hazel tied them, but kept the ropes loose.

Nora pressed the gun to the back of Hazel's head. "Tighter. Do you think I'm stupid?"

"Of course not. I have always believed in you, Nora." Hazel tightened the ropes.

"You're so gullible. This world isn't about the almighty Hazel Hoyt." She waved her gun at the empty chair. "Sit and don't try anything or I'll shoot your son."

Hazel obeyed.

Nora stuffed her gun into her waistband and extracted extra ropes from her pocket, tying Hazel to the chair. "Okay, now that you're all secure, I need to meet my love and make final preparations." She holstered her weapon and placed gags on Hazel's father and son.

"For what?" Hazel asked.

"Your burials, of course." Nora reached into her pockets and shrugged. "I guess I'm all out of gags, but don't worry. No one will hear you if you scream."

Another flash of lightning hit as Nora left the lookout.

Thunder exploded and shook the structure, elevating Hazel's terror.

Then she remembered the knife in her ankle holster. Nora had failed to check there.

But how could Hazel get to it?

Show me, Lord.

She had to get to Mitchell before Firebug did. "Dad, I tried to keep your ropes loose, as much as I could with Nora watching. Can you get out of them? There's a knife in my ankle holster. Get it and cut us loose. Hurry!" She stole a glimpse over her shoulder.

Her father wiggled his hands, working his way out of the ropes. Moments later, he succeeded and yanked his gag from his mouth. "I'm free." He untied his ankle restraints and bolted out of the chair. Circling around to Hazel, he lifted her pant leg and withdrew the knife, then cut her and Jackson free.

Hazel scooped her son into her arms. "Let's go."

Her dad held up the knife. "I'll go first. Stay close behind me."

They made their way out of the lookout and down the stairs.

Voices caught her attention. She had to look for Mitchell, but first she had to keep her son safe. She spied a dense row of bushes and pointed. "Dad, you hide with Jackson over there."

"No, Mama," Jackson cried. "Don't leave me."

Hazel set him down. "Baby, we will come back for you. I have to stop the bad people first. Can you be brave for Mama? Stay hidden with Grandpa."

A fat tear rolled down his cheek, and he nodded.

The duo crawled into the bushes. Her father turned and handed her the knife. "Take this and be careful. I have complete faith in you. Go."

She nodded and scrambled toward the voices, praying she wasn't too late.

Mitchell rode around the trail's last bend after following all of Hazel's buttercup-flower bread crumbs. The storm hadn't let up, and he was soaked. Chills attacked his body, but he pressed forward and rode toward the old park station lookout. A place he guessed the team had failed to check because of the tough terrain. He spotted Hazel's horse and veered Thunder over, stopping beside Chestnut. Mitchell dismounted and tethered his horse. He rubbed Chestnut's flank. "Buddy, glad to see you."

Mitchell's radio crackled, startling him. He was surprised it worked, but perhaps the elevation helped.

"Boomer—you—" Morgan's broken voice came through the radio.

Smoke wafted in the distance, and Mitchell knew why

his leader was calling. He unhooked the device from his belt and pressed the button. "Come again?"

"Fire—north—near—you."

Firebug had obviously set a fire close to the lookout to trap them all in case they got away. The fire would stop them from retreating down the mountain. How much could he tell his boss? After determining he was alone, Mitchell pressed the button. "I'm at Micmore Ridge and need to rescue Hazel. Send any help you can. Now!"

"Understood. Stay—alert. Found Smokey hiding—tracker—your radio. He figured out—identity. Firebug is—"

A branch snapped behind him and Mitchell turned.

A man's face came into view as he whacked Mitchell on the head with a shovel. A question tumbled through Mitchell's mind before he crumbled to the ground.

Firebug was Levi Dotson?

A noise jerked Mitchell awake. Dampness surrounded him in an enclosed area. Where was he?

A pile of dirt sprinkled on top of him.

NO! Not again.

He squirmed, trying to release the restraints on his hands bound in front of his face, but Firebug had positioned Mitchell on his side in a narrow, dug-out grave.

"You weren't supposed to wake up," Levi said. "Guess I didn't hit you hard enough."

Mitchell shifted his hands closer to his face. He had to block his nose and mouth if he was going to live. He struggled to turn to look at his assailant, his legs already covered with heavy, damp dirt. "Levi, why? I barely know you."

"Simple. You taught your team well. They are too good at putting out my fires, so I thought I'd cut the head off the snake—so to speak. You need to die for interfering with my plan of retribution."

Even in the murky daylight, Mitchell didn't miss the sneer on Levi's face. "Why Hazel and her son? Why Frank?"

"I had to give my love her retribution too. I'm getting married next month, and I promised a wedding gift for Nora."

Mitchell tried to kick himself free, but his tied feet prevented movement. "Nora Martin is your accomplice? Why?"

"Because she was unjustly treated by Frank Hoyt. Hazel shouldn't have gotten the warden's job. Nora deserved it." He dug his shovel into the ground and sprinkled another load of dirt into Mitchell's grave. This one landed on his chest.

When the rain of dirt stopped, he glanced up at Levi. "You need help. You kidnapped an innocent child."

"Children have to pay for the sins of their parents."

Lord, help me. I need to get out of here and save Hazel, Jackson and Frank.

He had to buy time. "Tell me, why start all these fires? Why kill firefighters?"

"Well, since no one is coming to save you, I'll tell you a story." He leaned on the shovel. "When I was a teenager, fires fascinated me. Even started a few, but then one went horribly wrong and our house caught on fire. I called 9-1-1. Firefighters took their sweet time getting there. Said the road was blocked, but it was just an excuse to cover up their blunder."

Mitchell knew from experience that was wrong. Often, heavy traffic or other roadblocks hindered their approach to the scene, but firefighters did everything in their power to save lives.

"By the time they got there and rescued me, the house's

top level was demolished. The chief pulled his team out and my parents died." He lifted his shirt and revealed hideous burn scars. "I not only paid the price with these horrid reminders but my mom and dad were gone."

"But you started the fire. Stop blaming others for your mistake!"

The man's face twisted into an evil expression. He lifted another shovel full of dirt, then another, and dumped them into the grave, filling the space on and around Mitchell's chest. "Don't tell me it was all me. That chief could have kept his team fighting longer. However, he's already paid with his life." He punched the shovel into the soil again. "Do you know how humiliating it was in gym class when I had to shower? Those boys made fun of my scars. That's when I realized all firefighters—including you and your team—would pay for what they did to me."

This man really had a warped perspective.

"Enough chitchat. Time to die." He shoveled in more dirt.

Mitchell turned his head. He had to shield his breathing, but it wouldn't be long before the dirt would cover his face and he'd succumb to the loss of air. He sputtered as Levi kept dropping dirt on his head.

"Now I need to dig your love's grave. Goodbye, Boomer." One last shovelful and Mitchell's world went black. Levi's words were a distant echo as Mitchell felt him pat the soil hard.

Then—silence.

He mumbled as loud as he could, but would anyone hear him?

Come back to God.

His sister's words filtered through the dirt and into Mitchell's mind, along with the realization he'd never see his sister or Hazel again. Never be able to tell Bree's best friend how he'd fallen for her.

I'm sorry, Hazel. I failed you.

Lord, I'm sorry for failing You too. Sorry for not trusting in You with all aspects of my life. For blaming You when I should have taken ownership. You were there all the time, and I missed Your presence. I surrender everything back to You. Take my life—whatever's left of it—and use it for Your glory.

Help Bree not to be sad. Tell her I'll see her again someday.

Lord, save Hazel, Jackson and Frank. Don't let them die.

Mitchell's breaths came in strained bursts as he fought to stay conscious. He yelled, but his words came out mumbled. It was no use. No one would hear him now.

Lord, I surrender to You.

His grave overtook him.

A muffled cry sounded around the bend. *Mitchell!* Hazel ran as fast as she could in the pelting rain. Thunder and lightning hammered Micmore Ridge, sending terror through her body. She stopped. *Give me strength. You've got this.* She inhaled and shot off like a dart toward the sound of his voice, with one thing on her mind. Save the man she loved.

She rounded the corner and noted a shovel stuck in a dirt mound. *No, Lord!* Had Nora and Firebug made good on their promise of digging their graves? Was Mitchell beneath that pile of soil? She didn't know for sure, but couldn't take the chance. She grabbed the shovel and dug.

Within minutes, she created an opening and dropped the shovel, digging with her hands until a soiled blue plaid shirt came into view. Mitchell.

Hazel changed her position to where she guessed his

head was and continued digging. His ashen face appeared. She brushed away the soil from his head and chest, turned his head toward her, and felt for a pulse.

Weak.

Lord, save him. Hazel moved dirt out of his mouth and gave him rescue breaths. Then waited.

Nothing.

"Come on, Mitchell! Come back to me." She gave him more breaths. Then waited.

He coughed and his eyes flew open.

"Thank God." Hazel helped clear the rest of the dirt off his torso and rolled him back to his side to expel anything else obstructing his airways.

Once again he coughed, then took a ragged breath. "You. Saved. Me."

She hauled him into her arms. "Of course I did."

"Get me out of here. We need to catch Levi." When she'd cleared the rest of the dirt away, he pushed on the ground to stand, but staggered.

She sprang upright and grabbed him around the waist. "Wait, Levi is Firebug?"

"I'll tell you more later. We have to find—"

"I'm right here," the voice said. "Well, well, well. The Hoyts have surprised me. I didn't think you had it in you, from what Nora told me about you, Hazel."

Hazel turned and faced the barrel of Levi Dotson's shotgun. "Nora fed you lies. All lies. I never did anything to hurt her."

"You're the liar." Nora walked out from behind a tree and pistol-whipped Hazel in the face.

Hazel stumbled backward but kept her balance.

Fire raged around them and slithered toward the lookout. All would be lost if they didn't act fast. *Lord, send more rain.*

Mitchell bulldozed into Levi, knocking him onto the ground as a shot rang out in the air before the weapon slipped out of Levi's hold. The two wrestled to gain ownership, rolling together down a small incline. Mitchell grabbed the weapon, knocking the butt end into Levi. He slumped, unconscious.

"No!" Nora yelled, raising her gun to shoot Mitchell.

Hazel held out the knife and stampeded toward Nora, ready to plunge the blade if need be. She would save those she loved.

The woman sidestepped Hazel's attack. "Nice try. See, I am better than you." She lifted her gun again, finger on the trigger.

Hazel was out of options.

"No!" Her father careened out of nowhere, bull-rushing toward Nora.

The gun went off and her father staggered and fell to his knees, holding his arm.

"Dad!" Hazel yelled.

Nora turned the gun at Hazel. "Your time is up, my *friend.*"

A shotgun blast pierced the morning air, sending a flock of birds into the sky.

And Nora to the ground.

Hazel glanced behind her.

Mitchell's shot had met his target.

Hazel stumbled over to her father. "You okay?"

"I'm fine. Get Jackson and get out of here. The fire's growing."

Pounding footfalls filled the area.

Hazel stood and turned in their direction.

"Boomer!" Kane yelled, running toward them with Mitchell's team close behind.

"Smokey, how did you know?" Mitchell asked.

"Tracker in your radio. Sorry for being MIA, but I was working secretly with the police to trap Levi once I figured out Firebug's identity. They wouldn't let me tell anyone." He raised his gear. "You take these folks to the bottom and get more help. We'll put out the fire."

"Thank you." Mitchell slapped his back.

Hazel drew her father to his feet. "Where's Jackson?"

"Mama!" Jackson yelled, appearing around the corner.

Hazel bent down and opened her arms.

Jackson ran into them. "You saved us. I knew you would."

Her father squeezed her shoulder and held his hand out to Mitchell. "Give me the shotgun. I'll hold it over Levi. You guys call for help and take shelter from the flames."

Mitchell handed over the weapon and nodded.

From where she stooped on the dirt hugging her son, Hazel called to him. "Mitch, this is Jackson."

Mitchell bent low and shook the boy's hand. "We're gonna be best buds."

Jackson's widened eyes gazed at Hazel as if questioning the man's statement.

"It's true." Hazel lifted her son. "Let's get to Chestnut. There's a radio in my saddle. We can call Stein and his men."

The group staggered down the hill, distancing themselves from the fire. Hazel retrieved her radio hidden in Chestnut's saddle and requested help.

"Hazel, I need to tell you something," Mitchell said.

She eyed her son. He sat on a rock under a tree, taking shelter from the rain. Safe and sound. Exactly where she needed him to be.

Hazel turned back to Mitchell, placing her finger on his lips. "Before you do, I need to tell *you* something. I'm sorry for the other night. You shared how you were feeling and I shut you out. I need to tell you why." She inhaled to give herself strength. "I made some mistakes in college. Fell in love… Well, thought I did. I'd fallen away from Christ and gave in to my boyfriend's pressures. After I found out I was pregnant, Jackson's father abandoned us, breaking my heart. I vowed then I would raise my son by myself. I didn't need a man to smash my dreams or hurt my son." She sighed. "Then you came back into my life and I fell for you all over again. Yes, you infuriated me when I heard you say you only thought of me as your little sister. I thought—"

He wrapped his arm around her waist and tugged her closer, silencing her with a kiss.

A kiss that literally took her breath away.

He pulled back. "Does that show you I don't think of you as a sister?"

She smiled. "I love you, Mitchell Booth."

"And I love you. I realized I had a crush on you when you were a kid following me around like a lost puppy dog."

She swatted him. "Did not. You—"

Once again, he silenced her with his soft lips on top of hers.

Jackson giggled and nestled himself between them, breaking them apart.

Hazel laughed and wrapped the men of her life in her arms, lifting her gaze to the sky. A cloud broke free and exposed the sun's rays as the smoke on the hill dissipated.

All was well again.

Not only was her relationship with her father restored but God had helped her finally put the past behind her, so she could move forward.

Anew.

EPILOGUE

Eighteen months later

Hazel crawled out from under her plush, buffalo plaid comforter and slipped out of bed. After wrapping a nearby blanket around her shoulders, she tiptoed to the door and glanced back at her husband of twelve months. She chuckled at Mitchell's light snore. They had married one year ago and begun their lives together with Jackson. And today… Hazel would tell her husband her new secret. But first, she'd make coffee and his favorite breakfast.

She shuffled down the cabin's hardwood corridor—their makeshift home on the land her parents had given to them as a wedding present. They'd live in the small structure until the ranch Mitchell promised her could be completed. He had sold his condo and they had plans to build a home similar to the Hoyt Hideaway Ranch, but not as big, and they'd already picked out a name. Second Chance Booth Refuge—a ranch experience for individuals wanting a new start in life. Like God had given Mitchell and Hazel.

Hazel entered her kitchen and prepared a pot of coffee, hoping the smell would draw her husband out of his deep sleep. As she whipped up a batch of pancakes, she thought over the events that had brought her and Mitchell together.

The Micmore Wildfire Unit had successfully extinguished the wildfires set by the Rocky Mountain Firebug. Levi Dotson had pled guilty to all charges and did it with a sneer on his face. Even after being sentenced for multiple fires and murders, the man still vowed to get retribution against firefighters from prison. He threatened both Mitchell and Hazel for killing his fiancée. Nora Martin had died from the gunshot wound. Mitchell underwent counseling for months after taking her life in self-defense.

Frank and Erica Hoyt had provided lodging for Vincent Taylor and helped him get back on his feet. He now lived with them at the Hoyt ranch and was reinstating his medical license—with Hazel's father's help. Meanwhile, he was employed at Micmore National Park as a medic. Snake and Jackson had bonded over their experience in the wilderness. Once the Booth ranch was ready, Snake would move onto their property—at Jackson's insistence—and Hazel agreed.

Hazel and her father had reconnected after their near-death experience. He had promised Hazel he'd try to mend all his relationships with his children.

Hazel poured the batter into the frying pan and waited for the pancakes to brown.

"What do I smell?" Mitchell entered the room and planted multiple kisses on the back of his wife's neck.

She hunched her shoulders. "That tickles." She turned and kissed him. "I'm making blueberry pancakes. Morning, love."

"Morning." He took a mug from the cupboard and poured in coffee. "What's the special occasion?"

"You'll find out."

"I thought we agreed on no more secrets." He sipped his coffee.

She smirked. "Oh, you'll like this one."

He tilted his head.

"Secrets?" Jackson entered the room, rubbing his eyes. "Who has secrets?"

"Your mother." Mitchell tousled the nine-year-old's hair. "Morning, bud."

Hazel gathered dishes and set the table. "Jackson, you washed up?"

He climbed into a chair. "Yup. Let's eat."

After a feast of blueberry pancakes and fresh maple syrup, Hazel poured herself another large cup of coffee. She peeked out the kitchen window. Daylight was almost upon them. She turned to her boys. "How about we sit out on the back deck?"

"Brrrr…" Mitchell faked a chill, rubbing his arms.

Jackson puckered up his lips and nose. "It's cold out there."

"Don't be babies. We're having a warm spell right now." Even though it was January in Alberta and normally cold, temperatures had risen and Hazel wanted to watch the sunrise from her favorite spot—the wooden swing on the wraparound porch. "Come on. Grab your coats. I'll meet you out there."

She picked up her coat and coffee cup, and walked through the patio doors. She sat on the swing and waited for the two men in her life.

Moments later, they appeared.

Hazel patted the spot beside her. "Mitch, sit."

He obeyed while Jackson plunked down in the rocker beside them.

Mitchell cupped his hands around his mug. "Okay, can you tell us your secret?"

Butterflies flapped their wings in her tummy as the excitement over her news elevated. She turned to face her husband and drew in a breath. "You're gonna be a father."

His eyes widened as he lowered the mug from his mouth. "You're pregnant?"

"That's what it means, my love." She kissed his forehead. "Are you happy?"

A tear glistened in his eye. "Of course I am." He brushed his lips over hers. "God is good."

"All the time." Hazel turned to Jackson. "Did you hear that? You're gonna be a big brother."

Jackson jumped up from the rocker and did a happy dance. "Yay!" He skipped back and forth along the porch.

Hazel guided her husband's face within inches of hers. "I love you with all my heart."

"Ditto. I praise God daily for bringing us together."

They kissed before leaning back on the swing, letting it glide as they watched the spectacular view from their deck.

The red-orange sun crested over the mountain, glistening the snow-capped peaks. Hazel let out a soft sigh and thanked God for helping her move forward in life by dealing with her past, forgiving and ultimately trusting in His perfect plan. The sun continued to rise as a verse in Lamentations flashed through Hazel's mind.

Through the Lord's mercies we are not consumed, Because his compassions fail not. They are new every morning; great is thy faithfulness.

Hazel grabbed her husband's hand and squeezed. *Yes, they are.*

* * * * *

Dear Reader,

I hope you enjoyed reading Hazel and Mitchell's story as much as I loved writing it. They both love the mountains and wilderness, so it was natural to put them together into a spine-tingling race against the clock. Plus I wanted to show their family relationship struggles, their journey of forgiveness, and realization they needed to put their pasts behind them in order to move forward. Something we all have to learn, right? Praise God that His faithfulness and mercies are new every day.

It was also fun to create the fictional mountains/wilderness and national park within the Rocky Mountains of Alberta. It is an absolutely stunning part of Canada. The mountains are majestic!

I'd love to hear from you. You can contact me through my website www.darlenelturner.com and also sign up for my newsletter to receive exclusive subscriber giveaways. Thanks for reading my story.

God bless,
Darlene L. Turner

COMING NEXT MONTH FROM
Love Inspired Suspense

UNDERCOVER OPERATION
Pacific Northwest K-9 Unit • by Maggie K. Black

After three bloodhound puppies are stolen, K-9 officer Asher Gilmore and trainer Peyton Burns are forced to go undercover as married drug smugglers to rescue them. But infiltrating the criminals will be more dangerous than expected, putting the operation, the puppies and their own lives at risk.

TRACKED THROUGH THE WOODS
by Laura Scott

Abby Miller is determined to find her missing FBI informant father before the mafia does, but time is running out. Can she trust special agent Wyatt Kane to protect her from the gunmen on her trail, to locate her father—and to uncover an FBI mole?

HUNTED AT CHRISTMAS
Amish Country Justice • by Dana R. Lynn

When single mother Addison Johnson is attacked by a hit man, she learns there's a price on her head. Soon it becomes clear that Isaiah Bender—the bounty hunter hired to track her down for crimes she didn't commit—is her only hope for survival.

SEEKING JUSTICE
by Sharee Stover

With her undercover operation in jeopardy, FBI agent Tiandra Daugherty replaces her injured partner with his identical twin brother, Officer Elijah Kenyon. But saving her mission puts Elijah in danger. Can Tiandra and her K-9 keep him alive before he becomes the next target?

RESCUING THE STOLEN CHILD
by Connie Queen

When Texas Ranger Zane Adcock's grandson is kidnapped and used as leverage to get Zane to investigate an old murder case, he calls his ex-fiancée for help. Zane and retired US marshal Bliss Walker will risk their lives to take down the criminals...and find the missing boy before it's too late.

CHRISTMAS MURDER COVER-UP
by Shannon Redmon

After Detective Liz Burke finds her confidential informant dead and interrupts the killer's escape, she's knocked unconscious and struggles to remember the details of the murder. With a target on her back, she must team up with homicide detective Oz Kelly to unravel a deadly scheme—and stay alive.

LOOK FOR THESE AND OTHER LOVE INSPIRED BOOKS WHEREVER BOOKS ARE SOLD, INCLUDING MOST BOOKSTORES, SUPERMARKETS, DISCOUNT STORES AND DRUGSTORES.

Get 3 FREE REWARDS!

We'll send you 2 FREE Books plus a FREE Mystery Gift.

FREE Value Over **$20**

Both the **Love Inspired®** and **Love Inspired® Suspense** series feature compelling novels filled with inspirational romance, faith, forgiveness and hope.

YES! Please send me 2 FREE novels from the Love Inspired or Love Inspired Suspense series and my FREE gift (gift is worth about $10 retail). After receiving them, if I don't wish to receive any more books, I can return the shipping statement marked "cancel." If I don't cancel, I will receive 6 brand-new Love Inspired Larger-Print books or Love Inspired Suspense Larger-Print books every month and be billed just $6.49 each in the U.S. or $6.74 each in Canada. That is a savings of at least 16% off the cover price. It's quite a bargain! Shipping and handling is just 50¢ per book in the U.S. and $1.25 per book in Canada.* I understand that accepting the 2 free books and gift places me under no obligation to buy anything. I can always return a shipment and cancel at any time by calling the number below. The free books and gift are mine to keep no matter what I decide.

Choose one:
☐ **Love Inspired Larger-Print**
(122/322 BPA GRPA)

☐ **Love Inspired Suspense Larger-Print**
(107/307 BPA GRPA)

☐ **Or Try Both!**
(122/322 & 107/307 BPA GRRP)

Name (please print)

Address   Apt. #

City   State/Province   Zip/Postal Code

Email: Please check this box ☐ if you would like to receive newsletters and promotional emails from Harlequin Enterprises ULC and its affiliates. You can unsubscribe anytime.

Mail to the Harlequin Reader Service:
IN U.S.A.: P.O. Box 1341, Buffalo, NY 14240-8531
IN CANADA: P.O. Box 603, Fort Erie, Ontario L2A 5X3

Want to try 2 free books from another series! Call 1-800-873-8635 or visit www.ReaderService.com.

---

*Terms and prices subject to change without notice. Prices do not include sales taxes, which will be charged (if applicable) based on your state or country of residence. Canadian residents will be charged applicable taxes. Offer not valid in Quebec. This offer is limited to one order per household. Books received may not be as shown. Not valid for current subscribers to the Love Inspired or Love Inspired Suspense series. All orders subject to approval. Credit or debit balances in a customer's account(s) may be offset by any other outstanding balance owed by or to the customer. Please allow 4 to 6 weeks for delivery. Offer available while quantities last.

Your Privacy—Your information is being collected by Harlequin Enterprises ULC, operating as Harlequin Reader Service. For a complete summary of the information we collect, how we use this information and to whom it is disclosed, please visit our privacy notice located at corporate.harlequin.com/privacy-notice. From time to time we may also exchange your personal information with reputable third parties. If you wish to opt out of this sharing of your personal information, please visit readerservice.com/consumerschoice or call 1-800-873-8635. **Notice to California Residents**—Under California law, you have specific rights to control and access your data. For more information on these rights and how to exercise them, visit corporate.harlequin.com/california-privacy.

LIRLIS23

HARLEQUIN
PLUS

Try the best multimedia subscription service for romance readers like you!

Read, Watch and Play.

Experience the easiest way to get the romance content you crave.

Start your **FREE TRIAL** at
www.harlequinplus.com/freetrial.